MAN PICKS FLOWER

Roger King

Regal House Publishing

Published by
Regal House Publishing, LLC
Raleigh, NC 27605

ISBN -13 (paperback): 9781646035663
ISBN -13 (epub): 9781646035670
Library of Congress Control Number: 2024935069

All efforts were made to determine the copyright holders and obtain
their permissions in any circumstance where copyrighted material was
used. The publisher apologizes if any errors were made during this
process, or if any omissions occurred. If noted, please contact the
publisher and all efforts will be made to incorporate permissions in
future editions.

Cover images and design by © C. B. Royal

Regal House Publishing, LLC
https://regalhousepublishing.com

Printed in the United States of America

To Celia

2015

J ohn woke to the thought—and this was a novel thought—
that it would brighten up the house, introduce new life
into the house, if he were to cut some flowers and bring
them inside. In the fifteen years since his retirement to New
Hampshire, he had not once brought flowers into his house,
nor had anyone brought flowers to him. But then never before
had the daffodils been so numerous. This new idea addressed
a vague sense that the old farmhouse had become less safe and
less his, and that he would do well to imprint himself upon it
in this new way.

In the middle of the yard, where they were most dense,
he stopped and bent over the daffodils. Half a dozen variet-
ies were thriving there, naturalized as promised fifteen years
earlier by the mail-order catalogue. The range of size, color,
and design was, now he looked more closely than he had ever
looked before, extraordinary. He selected one that particularly
struck him with its allure, cupping the flower with his left hand
while his right readied the scissors. Its petals were yellow but
the trumpet was white, shading into pink—no, more of an
orange; no, something in between—as it expanded towards the
top, which, now he looked even more closely, was not a simple
edge, but an elaborately layered frieze of thrilling complexity.
The flower opened up towards him, and with this evolved
seduction, halted him.

He stayed there, stooped and still, the thrum of aches
and pains that came with age no longer registering, the press
of memory less obviously pressing. Memory was, like the
surrounding forest, always wanting to overtake his hard-won
space, infant seedlings first, then the beguile of saplings, then
the great fact of trees. They would march down the scrub and

rock of his yard, overtake his shrubs and flowers, split open his house, his head.

Now that he was frozen in place, he had time enough to wonder if the freeze might be actual, since the unprecedented impulse to go out into the yard of his old New Hampshire farmhouse and cut flowers had led him into the cold air with just a cardigan, no hat, and thin slippers, through which he could feel the sog of snowmelt. But still he did not move, instead noting that not only were the daffodils more numerous than ever before, they were also earlier than ever before, and that if he plotted a graph over the last fifteen years it would show a progressive tendency towards earliness, which he supposed was the gentle announcement of a fast-warming planet—like a welcome breeze that presages a dangerous storm.

Out of a habit of mental rigor with which he reassured himself of his continued readiness for intelligence work, he ran through the order of events—the rise of science in ancient Greece, its refinement through the Middle East and back to Europe, on to the industrial revolution in Britain, the evident requirement of nascent capitalism for perpetual growth, the expansion of human population through agriculture and medicine, the revealed limitless appetite for consumption, the unfortunate ability to extract many millions of years of deposited biomass in a hundred, the eclipse of wise government by shallow business interests, the general absence of human humility in the face of nature—until he was satisfied that in the unlikely case that he was called to account, John Bradley would be able to explain the early daffodil resting in his palm, with its exuberantly ruffled opening. It really was a gorgeous thing and though intended to invite pollinating insects, it had also invited him, at which point thought was displaced by something like entrancement, a skipped page in existence, so that he was not aware of the relaxation of his muscles, nor the tears rising in him, not the utter joy of this emptiness.

When consciousness returned, it arrived into his undefended

space with locomotive speed and delivered to him three unwanted instances of bloom, three engulfing horrors: fire, blood, and spit. He was reminded that his life had been arranged so as to defend himself from such memories, and that refusal of feeling was its reasonable price. The first was an expanding yellow, shading into red, bordered by black: an explosion. The second was a woman's face, close and shocked white, bright blood erupting. The third was a girl moving up from below him to spit into his face. There were words accompanying the last. "Jim," they went, "you rape me." They were made more terrible, in that his name was John.

Time passed. He was cold and on his knees. He could not say what caused the skip in consciousness, and he wondered if this was a stroke, or perhaps his brain had become too cold for ordered thought. Now, he scrambled to put himself back on a path of present purpose, quickly snipping the stem of the lovely daffodil that he still held, dimly aware as he did so that before the lapse of consciousness there briefly had been something wonderful. He made a pass at looking for this lost happiness, but quickly abandoned the search because of the dangerous proximity of shame. The aching joints, which he had forgotten, made themselves felt again, the old injury to his left shoulder took up its customary throb, and a headache was growing, so that he willfully suppressed all present sensation and applied himself to standing and to cutting more blooms to achieve a vase full. He brushed aside the thought that he had chosen to bring life into his house by means of little executions.

Harry was already dressed, the too-sleek suit back on, last night's tie folded into a side pocket, his late brother's soft black moccasins suspended from the fingertips of his left hand. Deva was still splayed asleep, sheets tangled between her legs, her face illuminated by the street lights of Bloomsbury, the King's Cross end. He regarded her and started to seek words to describe her beauty, then stopped himself. The night had been both elating and sickening, comfort found where he had imagined doing harm. We hail from opposing poles of modesty, he thought, Brazil and Pakistan. Londoners. He would sort it out later.

Deva had requested that he leave early, before her daughter, Nadia, might wake. Now, at five, it was still only six hours since they had first spoken, only two months since he learned of her existence. The information had been offered to him on the understanding that he might want to act on it. Dreams passed visibly beneath Deva's eyelids. She was asleep with her arms spread wide, undefended.

He considered the photo he held in his right hand. In it, an elderly man in a beige cardigan was bending attentively over a splash of bright daffodils set in a rocky landscape bordering a forest. The man was alone. The photo was taken from behind so that the face was not visible. Leaving the photo for Deva, without any explanation, made no sense, unless further confusion was the antidote to confusion. It was an impulse he did not want to investigate. He let the photo fall onto a cluttered, low table, where it might or might not be noticed, might or might not have been dropped by accident.

Passing the doorway to Nadia's room, he saw Deva's face again, decades younger. Nadia too had thrown aside the covers and flung her arms open to the world. Last night he had carried the sleeping child upstairs, her sweet spittle darkening the lapel of his suit. He now trod the stairs silently and eased the front door closed, leaving himself no way to return. On the short walk to where he had left his brother's Porsche, he slowed, trying to rouse anger against the damp pavement's argument for sadness. Dawdling back towards the family home—now his home— on Baker Street, his mind returned to his recent life in Deva's bed and the clatter of his contending selves. There was little traffic so that he was surprised to see a car following close behind. There had been nothing in his mirrors, and now there was this. It had arrived fast, but then he had been going slowly. Now the car swung past to dive in front, an arm of confident authority out the passenger window commanding him to stop. Not obviously a police car. No obvious reason for being stopped. The young man and woman who now energetically opened their doors were not uniformed, but were somehow familiar.

Jerked out of reverie, his brain raced. It first reminded him, unhelpfully, that he was a poet, and therefore out of place. Then it offered the shallow observation that he was driving a Porsche and that the car that had dived in front of him was a Volkswagen. As the two athletic young people hustled towards him, he slipped the car into reverse, then into forward, accelerating hard down a side road. His late brother's car obediently entered a new dimension of speed. Not designed for deliberation, it took its inexperienced driver into its exceptional world without his full permission. He was aware of the speedometer registering a hundred, aware of successfully making a left turn at a speed that should not be possible, and aware that, astonishingly, the Volkswagen was in sight behind him. He flung the car into the one-way street to his right, immediately flooring the accelerator, leaving himself no time to make sense of the iron builder's skip blocking the half of the road into which the car was pouring itself at catastrophic speed. There was an enormous life-denying noise. Then a long nothing.

By mid-afternoon, Deva's girlfriends had left the University College café in Bloomsbury, the Iranian to her children, the Scot to her thesis, and finally the Bangladeshi to a shockingly wicked assignation, about which she felt comfortable confiding only in Deva. The search for a job had foundered on Deva's disinclination towards any of the possibilities on offer. Everyone would want the junior academic posts, which really were not worth having, while post-doctoral research grants meant the sad prolonging of a student persona. All the others jobs—the ones plastered on the real and virtual notice boards—were menial, and as badly paid as singing to Brazilian exiles at the Miranda nightclub, without any of the satisfactions.

She bought a second coffee, found a spot away from others, put on her glasses, and settled into a book of such thickness that those who noticed her might think that both book and glasses were conscious accessories, gilding a lily already too conspicuously gilded. In fact, she was soon fully lost to the tome on *structuralisme*, surrendered to that part of her that was ravenous for intellect and the relief that it offered from all that was personal.

"You're Deva?" a voice asked, apparently with little doubt. Reluctantly, Deva looked up, a finger pressed on the sentence being read. The speaker was a stocky Englishwoman with sensibly short gray hair. A stranger.

"Yes," she conceded.

"Professor Grinnell thought I might find you here."

"Did he?" Professor Grinnell, Deva thought, took far too much interest in her whereabouts.

"Yes. Mrs. Slater. Sally Slater. It's about a job. He thought you might be interested." She did not offer her hand.

"Mrs. Slater?"

"Yes, Sally Slater. The professor thinks very highly of you, you know. Do you mind if I sit down?" And she sat, or rather perched. "If you have a few minutes."

"A few," said Deva. She kept her finger on her book to mark both her place and the present allocation of her minutes. A job was good. A job beholden to Professor Grinnell, maybe not so good.

"I can't say very much today. I know that sounds odd, but later you'll understand why. What I can tell you is that the job is here in London, that it will use your anthropology background in an unusual way, and that it will pay more than most academic work. Probably more than your present job at the nightclub, although I only have the professor's opinion on that. I don't know the nightclub world very well. I imagine there might be tips. But you're a mother and I would suppose a flexible daytime job could suit you. Or, if you wished, you might be able to do both."

"He told you all this about me?"

"Well, yes. Mostly. I had to do a little research because of the special nature of the work. Again, later you'll understand why. I'm so sorry to have caught you by surprise and without proper introduction, but there is some urgency. Oh, I should also say that if you are offered the job, you will be doing good. You'll be helping someone who very much needs your help."

"So, you are not actually offering me a job."

"There has to be an interview. Two really. You have to meet your employer, who is also in a way mine. But I know you would be highly favored. I wonder, could you possibly come tomorrow? To this address. I wrote instructions on the back. I believe you are free between seven and eight-thirty—your daughter's ballet class?"

Deva raised an eyebrow and turned the card over in her hand—just an address on one side, and handwritten instructions on the other. Apparently, there were doorbells and stairs that she would have to get right.

"It's an extraordinary home. It will surprise you." Mrs. Slater rose. "Can I say you'll be there?"

"A home. Not the university then?"

"Oh no. I should have made that clear. Not at all. Professor Grinnell is just by way of introducing ourselves to you. In case you have doubts, he'll vouch for us. Just as he vouched for you."

"Okay, but who is *us*?"

"I know. It's a bit silly. I'm representing someone who, by way of disability, can't presently represent himself. Someone I'm confident you will want to help. It will all make sense tomorrow. Can I say you'll come?"

Deva replied to Sally Slater's level look with a level look, then shrugged. "Why not? You'll be there?"

"I was sure you would. Yes, I'll be there. And just one last thing, Deva, could you keep this to yourself? An important part of this job would be your discretion."

"Really? I think I'm better known for my indiscretion."

"Well, yes, there is some irony in that."

"If I ask anything else, you're going to tell me I'll be told tomorrow, aren't you?"

"Yes, I'm afraid so. Exactly."

Notes to Future Self:

Your name is Harry.

This is your home. It belongs to you.

You are in London, England.

Mrs. Slater looks after all your needs.

There is nothing to be afraid of.

There have been other days like this day.

Your days are good. You forget them each night.

Your brain was injured in a car crash. You must keep calm.

Dr Elliot is your doctor.

Other people remember the past. You do not.

No one can tell you about your past. Do not ask.

One day your memory will return.

You become ill if you leave the house.

You have no family.

You may think you have a girlfriend, but you do not.

At the bottom of this toothpaste-splattered sheet of paper tucked into his bathroom mirror were some scribbles that were crossed out as no longer relevant. Now, Harry picked up the pencil and with intense concentration wrote a new one for the next morning's self: *A friend from before will visit you for the first time. Her name is Deva. You will not recognize her. She is coming to help you.*

Sleep was calling him now. His brain was closing down. But while he finished cleaning his teeth, Harry kept his eyes focused on the new addition to his list, this news just received, fearing that his writing might disappear overnight and this promise for his future with it.

1982

The girl, the spit, the accusation of rape, were from 1982, thirty-three years ago. Brazil. It was a memory of shame from the life of a young man that had since been overtaken by such an ocean of experience that it no longer could be readily discovered, except when exposed by the very lowest of tides.

The brief assignment to Brazil had been a crucial first test for John, before a longer, more responsible, overseas posting. The mission itself was of no great importance. For cover, John was simply a visiting employee of the US Agency for International Development, engaged in identifying possible projects on the Amazon fringe, where rich ranchers, poor settlers, and indigenous tribes contended over vast areas of potential riches. USAID cover had a history with Brazil's military governments, and his wife, Tania, was quick to remind him that an earlier project had been to teach the generals' police how to torture. John had replied wearily, "That was then."

"Travel to exotic lands, meet exciting new people, and kill them," she taunted.

John sighed that this was a worn-out cliché and he would not be killing anyone. Saving people was more like it. He could not tell her more. Then, in almost his last words to his wife before he left, he said, "Freedom doesn't come free," which sounded false and cheap, and beneath him.

John was a junior employee then. Far from playing any big global game, he took orders that were not referred to his judgment as to their merit. He argued to Tania that to gain influence for good, one first needed to gain seniority. She had scorned this as cowardice and delusion, with none of their youthful ideals to be found in it.

It was true that the security services and police in Brazil

were sometimes assassins. But Brazil under the generals in the eighties was, John judged, a different and more hopeful place than Brazil under the generals in the sixties. His job was to go to Concordia, where deforestation was a source of conflict and a reported opportunity for communist insurgence. He would establish contacts and monitor what was going on politically, and what might be at stake for US interests. He was told that a Brazilian botanist undertaking an inventory of Amazonian flora with American funding had gone missing and this could be a further pretext for his enquiries. He would have a jeep and a Brazilian government counterpart. His cover was a baggy aid program called, Development of Amazonia. If he actually identified some promising projects, that would be a useful bonus. "You'll be working on your own," he was told. "We'll see what sort of field man you make."

John, known to the Brazilians as Jim, was the only American in Concordia. His government counterpart was a bleary drunk who spoke some English and who had, in an earlier army career, visited the School of the America's in Georgia to learn to fight communism by any means necessary. Together they made tours of the surrounding areas in John's Jeep. His counterpart's preference was to visit the homes of rich ranchers and to ask about the missing botanist while enjoying food and drink. There were no leads. Everyone agreed that the Amazonian forest was dangerous for a man alone, even an experienced man. Anything might happen. He might turn up, or he might never be heard of again. Stonewalled, John acted out his cover by making increasingly pointless trips to the villages of migrant settlers and into the forest itself. On one of these he was shown a thatched house that was the site of a massacre. An indigenous family had been murdered and their home burned. "Who did this?" John asked carefully. "Of course," his counterpart replied, smiling, "it is the communists."

John quickly understood that there was no communist plot, just poor people who needed land, or who were in the way. He reported back to the US consulate office in Rio that he could find no trace of the missing botanist. The violence, he wrote, originated with a loose militia of ex-policemen whose leader had been trained by the US in counter-insurgency. They were financed by ranchers and loggers to assert their claims over the forest. Their political protection went from the local elite to the very highest levels of the military government. Opposition, he reported, was disorganized, but sometimes supported by Catholic priests and nuns. It did not constitute a destabilizing political force. He was told to make friends with the leaders of the militia, and to stay for another month.

Coming back to Concordia each afternoon, after going through the motions of looking for opportunities for economic development, John went to the least rough bar in town, which by any larger standard was still a rough bar, home to drunks and prostitutes and occasionally to fights between men taut with violent habits. For company, he had his dogged government counterpart along with some of the ex-policemen who worked for the ranchers, their women, and a couple of alcoholic locals who knew some English. Apart from this rough crew, he was alone.

The bar opened on to the ragged main street and he established a customary seat that gave him a view up and down the road, from which vantage point he noticed on several days a girl in a white blouse and blue skirt—a school uniform, he supposed—hurrying past, always alone, eyes always straight ahead against the stare of the men. She was pretty and neat, light-footed and purposeful. Tall for Concordia, where most people seemed to be short. Sixteen or seventeen, he guessed. He was not an expert on teenagers, especially teenagers in Brazil. His own daughters were four and six. He did not see any other children in the school uniform. She was out of place—too brisk, too fresh, for the town. He started to watch out for her. He imagined protecting her.

John's bar companions interpreted his increasingly morose disposition according to their own lights, and offered to fix him up with women. "You're a young man. You can afford the best, the youngest. You shouldn't go to bed alone. That's not our way." But he did not want the prostitutes who were pointed out to him, or even the non-prostitutes, who, according to his companions, might make an exception in his case. He thought of his daughters in Iowa. He thought of Tania who had, on his last visit home, refused to sleep with him because he was no longer the man she had married. He could not say that she was wrong.

John's abstinence made his companions uncomfortable. They wanted him to take a local woman to make him one of them, a regular man, a corruptible man they could trust. When he continued to decline their offers, one taunted, "Jim, is it that you are afraid of your wife?"

The way his eyes followed the girl was noted. The drunks and spongers and killers were pleased to find this common humanity in him. Their American wanted something they could give him: a girl. They were certain that his attention was lust and pointed this out to him.

When John protested, "I just like to see that girl," they laughed at this denial of a basic, universal truth. "No," he insisted, "I wonder about her. She's always alone. She doesn't look like she belongs here."

His counterpart held up his hand to silence the others and then made a deliberate reply. He said, "That girl is not from here. In fact, I do not know why she is here." John waited for more, and it came. "Maybe you should wonder about her. She's the daughter of the man you're looking for."

"He brought his daughter with him? Here? Why didn't you tell me?"

"You were looking for a man, not a girl. She shouldn't be here."

"She must be terrified. You should have told me. I have daughters of my own. Who's looking after her?"

The counterpart shrugged. "Many men here are willing to look after her."

Someone observed, "Every girl is someone's daughter. But

we still want them. Even this girl"—and the man squeezed his prostitute's breast—"is a daughter."

His companions warmed to their concern for John's welfare. They argued that the girl—alone, and in need of his protection—was a natural opportunity for him. She was, they joked, what he said he was looking for, a Brazilian natural resource going to waste.

The rules are different here, John reminded himself. Morality is always relative, never absolute. The American frontier had been just as rough. Don't judge the culture, was the first lesson of the field.

The next time he took his seat at the bar, his counterpart had a report. "That girl you want. She lives alone. She's still waiting for her father. Stupid."

"Why stupid?"

"It's been weeks."

"You think he's dead?"

He shrugged. "The jungle is dangerous. And this botanist made people uneasy. What if he said the forest was full of rare plants and should never be cut down?"

"Then, how is she managing?"

"She has a big lock on her door."

"I mean, if she has no family here, how does she manage?"

"How do pretty girls manage? Maybe you can help her. Sugar daddy. To replace the missing daddy."

"Not that sort of help," said John.

His counterpart leaned forward to push his point. "Then what sort of help, Jim? Are you just going to give her money for nothing? She wouldn't even understand. It would frighten her. She'd be hitting her head thinking, What does this man want from me? Doesn't he like me? What does he think he's buying with his money? She wouldn't trust you. Or she'd think, Maybe he can't even be a man. If you fuck her, then everything will make sense and she'll take your help." The counterpart was being an earnest cultural advisor now. "This is not America.

This is not even Rio. This is Concordia. Here, to refuse you would be an insult, an insult to me, the government, even to America. She can't do it. Just ask her. Or don't even ask. Make it simple, just take. Let me tell you, the innocent-looking ones are the worst. They sell their innocence again and again." He was pleased with this and laughed. "That one can make a fortune from her innocence."

"She goes with men?"

"A girl her age? Believe me, even the ugly ones. Think of it as a favor to her—you'll be saving her from the rest of us."

John waited for a day when his bar advisors were not around to witness his approach to the girl. She came to an abrupt stop in the street, the look of consternation on her face ready to slip towards terror, so that he spent an earnest minute assuring her in his poor Portuguese of his good intentions, his concern for her safety, his prior knowledge that her father was missing and his concern about that, of his own status as a father of daughters, and of the lack of decent people in this town. He said that he knew she also did not belong there, and might need help.

When he ran out of words she stared silently into his face, as if looking for the hidden trigger that would make her turn and run. Finally, she had dropped her head and, not looking directly at him, asked, "Can you find my father?"

"I'm trying," he said.

Her name was Veronica and John did renew his enquiries about her father. Heads were shaken. He had been auditing the flora of the forest, making lists of what he found and the products known by the indigenous people to be useful, just a botanist from the government department responsible for natural resources. This was his usual work, Veronica explained. He loved it. When she was smaller, her father had taught botany at a high school, but for years now he had traveled all over the country recording plants. He loved the forest and loved to work in it alone. Sometimes, if she pleaded, he took Veronica along, and she had come to love Amazonia too. But on this trip, he needed to go deeper for a day or two and had refused to take her.

John was convinced that people knew more than they were saying. A man cataloguing the value of the forest was a nuisance to the men intent on cutting it down, and those men paid and armed the thugs. Veronica's father had walked into the forest, and into a war. "The forest is always dangerous," was all John's counterpart would say. He told Veronica that no one had seen her father, but that he had instructed everyone connected with his project to look for him. "Thank you," she said, and hung her head.

The place where Veronica was staying, when John finally saw it, turned out to be a small, square one-story house. Her father had paid the rent in advance. There was one bedroom—her father's—a living room with a thin mattress on the floor made up with a sheet and a pillow—hers—and a simple kitchen with a gas ring for cooking. Water came from a communal tap. The toilet was outside, built around a hole in the ground. Veronica had not moved into the bedroom with its inviting double bed; it was waiting for her father's return. The house had been built recently and cheaply. There was an unfinished gesture towards surrounding it, and its neighboring twin, with a wall, but this embellishment had been abandoned.

Inside, everything was sparse and clean. Veronica's schoolbooks were piled precisely parallel to the edge of the dining table. The cup and plate she used were washed and ready to be used again. A full bucket of water was under the sink, covered by a cloth. While John took all this in at a single sweep, Veronica hesitated behind him in the doorway, then locked the door from the inside and stood with her back to it, frowning as she studied John studying the room. She had let a man into the house and was uncertain as to whether this was wise. Her father would have forbidden it, but until she found him, he could not forbid anything.

John asked, "What do you eat?"

"My father bought rice before he left. I was buying fish."

John nodded, looking at the little stove. "Where do you keep your rice?"

"It's nearly gone. He said he would only be away for two nights."

"You've money for food?"

She shook her head. "Not anymore."

"I'll give you some. You have to eat."

Veronica looked at him, then at her toes. "Why?"

"Why? Because you need it."

"Lots of people need food. Why me?"

"Your father was working for us. Indirectly. And you're a girl on your own in a strange town."

"If you find my father, I will not be alone. Would you still help me if I wasn't pretty? I don't want you to help me because of that."

John thought about this, and knew that part of a truthful answer was that he was charmed by her. He said, "I don't want anything from you, Veronica. Please trust me. I have daughters of my own. You're in trouble and you're in a rough town. Where's the rest of your family? Where's home?"

"Rio."

"It's a long journey. Expensive. And dangerous."

"I'm not going home. I know my father. He'll come back. He will not like that I let you in."

"But for now, you're alone. So just take this for food." He put a few notes on to the table. "It's not much. We're looking for your father."

She did not move towards the money.

"Do you have any idea which direction he went?"

"Just that it was into the forest. He knows how to be in the forest. He knows a lot about the plants. He loves the forest and it loves him. That's why I know he will come back."

John said, "You father sounds like a wonderful man," but his heart had sunk, knowing who else was in the forest and how little love was in them. He said, "I'd enjoy meeting him."

"You'll like him," replied Veronica.

John looked at her, young, graceful, and brave, and did want to help. There was the part of him that wanted to help her, which he recognized as good and decent, and which he was pleased to find still fully alive in him. Then there was the professional part of him that required collaboration with violent thugs in the service of some vague long-term benefit to his country that would be furthered by accommodating allies of the generals. He was part of his country's long involvement in Brazil that might reasonably be held responsible for the fate of Veronica's father. He said, "For now, you'll take the money. As a loan if you like. Your father can pay me back when he returns."

"Okay," replied Veronica, in English.

He stepped towards the door and she moved quickly to work the locks and open it. She had been worried that he would not leave.

John now wanted, above all, to help Veronica. His mind would no longer do the work of ideology, giving abstract political aims authority over him. If a kernel of decency was to survive, it was essential that he do his best for Veronica, and that he receive nothing in return. He might not deserve love, but he hoped he could give a little, and so keep his heart alive. Tania had retreated back to her roots in Iowa, wanting nothing from him. She made it clear that he had used up the store of her respect, and that love had vanished with it, along with the ability to bear his touch. This girl was only sixteen, poised in age between wife and daughters, an adult, yet with a heart still pure. In Concordia, where adulthood came early and purity was rare, a little love could count for a lot.

He took to going to Veronica's house every evening in preference to the bar, or the crummy hotel in town where he was lodged. She cooked simple food bought with the money he gave her, and after dinner they pored over her school books, keeping her mind off other things, and making sure that when she returned to Rio, she would not have fallen behind her classmates. She did not want to disappoint her father when he reappeared to sweep up his daughter and cast his appraising eye over her school work.

John was careful never to touch, though their heads were often close, poring over a single book, and the scent of Veronica did not, if he was rigorously honest, affect him in the same way as the scent of his own daughters. It was sweet and musky, cut with sex. While Veronica concentrated, he was sometimes captured by the neatness of her ears, or the arch of her slender neck. His tenderness towards her, as he watched her effort to concentrate while she was near tears, made him want to take her in his arms to comfort her, but he dare not. He knew there was confusion in him.

It was the domesticity of their arrangement that he treasured most: a meal cooked for him, the sitting down at a table with a graceful woman—no, girl—then later undertaking some small masculine chores to maintain the functioning of the house, and so receive gratitude for his efforts. There was nothing else like this in his life now, not even in America, where Tania tolerated him, he thought, only because she needed his income and her children might need a father

While John held himself in check, Veronica also stiffly held herself at a correct remove. She knew the power of her proximity. For years, men had been staring at her—admiring, imagining, graphically describing—and she had learned to look straight ahead in the street, and not to hesitate in her progress. She knew that when she leaned over the table and her hair fell forward, her neck showed to advantage. Before John arrived each evening, she fussed over how high her blouses should be buttoned—too high and too low might both be suggestive— and whether that night to wear her jeans or a skirt, and then the long skirt or the shorter one. She washed more carefully with the proximity to John in mind, aware of the perspiration that would soon soak them both in the tin-roofed house, and how close they would sit while John helped her with her math problems, or competed with her in the identification of plants, where she was more the teacher. She knew that their hands never touched, and vaguely understood that if touching meant nothing, they would naturally have done so. And she was aware that for both of them the high point was the English lesson, the only subject that licensed direct eye contact, produced humor, and which could cause in either of them a stumbling forgetfulness. Veronica felt the tension in John, and knew what it was, and that it cost him something to ignore it, but was too inexperienced to calculate how much, or whether this effect was good or bad. She always made sure her underwear was clean, arguing to herself that she always kept her underwear clean anyway, and that nothing could ever happen that would involve it being seen.

The quiet evenings together—John's regular report of no news about her father, their dinner, schoolwork, John's brisk departure at a modest hour—were, below the calm surface routine, a confusion of man and woman, father and child, giver and receiver, protector and protected, restraint and provocation. And, even deeper beneath the surface, there was buried John's suppressed understanding that if Veronica's father were dead, he might well have been killed by the men with whom he spent his days, his official allies, and that it might be this death that was permitting these quiet, domestic evenings of noble restraint. To Veronica, he was simply Jim of the USAID Development of Amazonia project, looking for new ways to do good.

He refreshed his enquiries about Veronica's father, hoping for evidence of life, not death. His counterpart gave him a sort of answer. "Jim, you need to listen. That government surveyor you keep asking about. Forget him. The girl's a sexy young cunt, but she should go home. There are other girls." Nobody for a second imagined that John's relationship with Veronica was chaste.

"You mean, he's dead?"

"I mean, you don't need to know. This is Brazil business,

Jim. We welcome your advice and assistance—thank you—but not on this. For the girl's sake, send her home. She will never see her father again. He wasn't part of anyone's plan."

Now that the fact of the death of Veronica's father was impossible to deny, and the safety of Veronica herself was in doubt, John was moved beyond pleasure, and was no longer able to suppress a sense of self-disgust. One evening, he went to her house, and stayed in the doorway, though the smell of dinner was reaching him. He said: "Veronica, I've talked to everyone I can about your father. It's time you went home to your mother. I will need to leave soon, and you're not safe in this town without me."

"You've heard something!" She was ready to cry.

"No, nothing. But if he's injured, maybe broke a leg, and is being looked after in the forest, it could be months before he works his way back. We don't know. But you know what this town is, and you should leave. In any case your mother must be worried about you. I can let you know if there's any news. Is there anyone who can come to fetch you?"

"Only my mother. Jim, please come inside!" She had been looking anxiously over his shoulder.

Reluctantly, John went to the table and sat, while she tended to the locks.

Veronica did not want to leave Concordia. It would confirm the hopelessness of her father's case. Also, she did not want to leave Jim, her placeholder father, a miraculous friend armed with the power to help. She was not prepared for a second loss.

John described a plan. Her mother could travel by bus to Altamira. The roads were good that far and there were no dangers. His own driver, a man he trusted, would drive her there to meet her mother. He'd arrange for an armed police escort, just to make sure. It was normal practice. And she must let him know how to contact her in case there was any news of her father. He was sickened to hear himself say it, but still said, "Of course, personally, I will be sad to see you go."

Veronica did not press him about her father. The silence hung between them. John was unable to hold her eye, which Veronica took as proof of a closeness to tears similar to her own. She composed herself, and said, "Thank you, Jim. You are good," at which, tears did well into John's eyes, offering Veronica further evidence of goodness.

She came around the table to where he sat, his eyes welling at the unbearable cumulation of his losses—his self-respect, his wife, this pure young woman he adored. Veronica, like a mother now, stood in front of him and gently let alight a hand upon his shoulder. He covered it with his own. "I'll miss you," she said. In reply, he nodded, and touched her cheek with the back of his free hand, then lifted her hair to push it behind her ear, the way she did herself when writing in her school books, then released it to its fall. She took his withdrawing hand and now held it in both of hers bringing it to her face. The scent of her underarms reached him.

Veronica said, in a steady voice, "Jim, I owe you so much. Every man I have met in this town has tried to have me. You had the opportunity, and you didn't try." She leaned over and darted her lips down towards his face, her aim amateurish.

John turned his head aside to easily evade her, then shook it, no, then looked up at her face, where embarrassment was coloring her, so that he instead nodded, yes. He did not know what sort of kiss she had intended, or whether she knew, the kiss of the daughter, or the lover, one grateful to have received, or one eager to give. Now, bending over, she held his head firmly in both of her hands and brought her lips down to his. He responded to this clarity, by raising his face then placing a hand to her nape to keep her there, while lips started to move in exploration and Veronica opened her mouth in an inexperienced girl's understanding of what an adult kiss might be, releasing in them both the force of long frustration. She let herself be excited so that responsibility would not be quite hers and even sadness might for a moment be obliterated. John's hand found her breasts and exposed them to the gaze of a man. She let them be exposed. She gasped when John's mouth took in a nipple and his tongue moved across it in miniature abrasion. This was what it was to be made love to by a man; her body wanted it.

It was easy to descend from the chair to Veronica's mattress on the floor. John did not know where this would end and would not think of it, because he could not bear for this to end. The tension and unhappiness of weeks were released in both of them. Veronica removed her blouse to avoid its damage, and then barely resisted the hand between her legs—it was silly to resist now, unfair almost, childish—where John thought he found a further permission, further confirmed by Veronica's gasp and grip when his finger slipped inside her. Her mouth was locked on his now, her arms tight around him, so that all that was occurring below her waist might be considered separate from the conscious Veronica, and deniable. John was poised over her, poised to enter her, his amazed eyes holding her eyes, waiting for an answer to his silent question, their bodies slick with sweat in the tropical heat. Veronica's reply was in the hips that raised to meet him, the sharp pain of his entry making her blurt, "No!" even as she encircled him more tightly with her arms, and locked her hands behind him, crying out again, as if in both lament and celebration at a whole world lost, while John gave in to her fierce arrest, wanting over all else, over all the horror, a victory for love. This was love, and beauty and goodness, offered with the authority of heaven, and he would accept. Veronica was intent now, shocked out of mind at the discovery that the offer of a simple kiss could lead to this, and transported by it. She had relied on John's proven restraint, hadn't she, his age, his experience, to keep her safe, so that when, soon, amid the intense flooding of new sensations, both painful and compelling, he had shuddered and groaned in helplessness, and come inside her, then collapsed within her strong embrace, she was abruptly returned to consciousness, knowing what she absolutely could not be expected to know in the confusion of passion, that this man was after all like other men, who wanted to fuck her and use her and leave her. In the shocking awareness of her part in this, and anger at her own naivety, and a further anger that it could not now all be taken back, and now remembering her father, and how she should be sad, she opened her eyes and saw John looking down on her with a stupid smile of happiness, as if this was simple and good, not the consequence of misery, so that without knowing why, without thought or sense or meaning, she drew back and spat into his face—part disgust, part slap, part play, part kiss— and said, in a refusal of her part that was in part jest, but also because she was, after all, a girl and he was a man, and she had the right, she said, in English, "Jim, you rape me!"

2015

The instructions to Deva from Mrs. Slater were to ring the bell labeled *Top* outside a mansion block, upon which a doorman would admit her. She should then take a lift to the sixth floor, and from there climb a short flight of steps to a black door marked *Roof*, where she should ring again, and would be met.

In the event, the roof door clicked open as Deva approached it without any sign of human presence, so that she found herself decanted into the evening air, alone. In front of her, as if this was earth not roof, there was a pathway of flat stones charmingly encroached upon by plants and shrubs and curving upwards towards the glass doors of a low modern building that sprawled across the old mansion block's expanse of rooftop in a complex crystal elegance. It was some architect's dream. The house lorded it over the neighboring buildings but was set back behind a parapet so as to be invisible from the street. As predicted by Mrs. Slater, Deva was surprised.

Mrs. Slater and a thinner, taller figure—a man—were standing motionless behind glass doors, looking down on Deva while she climbed the shallow steps towards them. She felt at a disadvantage and did not much care for this, so that she took time to turn away and take in the city view, a gesture of insouciance that rewarded her with actual spectacle, the darkening sky, the moon, and all the lights of London. The moment caught both Deva's breath and her attention, and thus returned her to herself. She took a moment, then resumed her climb, singing quietly.

Inside, she was immediately ushered by Mrs. Slater through a grand, open space into a small white office that showed no signs of regular use. There was a modern table with high-backed chairs around it.

"Deva, please sit," instructed Mrs. Slater, taking the chair next to her. The man had walked ahead and was already sitting opposite. "This is Dr Elliot," Mrs. Slater declared, as if no further explanation was required.

"Deva," said Deva.

"Of course," said Dr Elliot. "Thank you for coming. Mrs. Slater thinks you might be able to help us." He looked Deva up and down in a way that suggested that he might be inclined to take issue with this judgement.

"All I was told was there's someone who needs help. And somehow, it's a job for an anthropologist."

"Yes. I'll explain. It's a unique assignment." Dr Elliot now stood, as if his visual assessment of Deva was complete and for clarity of mind he needed to look elsewhere. He stood by the window, gazing out over the glow of London and the black night sky.

"I am a neurologist," he began. "Some months ago, a patient of mine was in a very serious car crash. His recovery has been excellent in most respects. Physically he has returned to good health, but he sustained significant brain damage. He was in a coma for a month, and after he first emerged, he twice fell back into a coma again and nearly died. He's fragile. Consciousness, in some sense, proved too much for him. But he is doing much better and, within the controlled environment we provide him, leads an almost normal life. Except in respect to memory. His long-term memory has not returned. He doesn't know who he is. This is my area of specialization."

Deva, now free to observe Dr Elliot, was making judgements. He was a man apparently unconcerned with making an impression. His suit and tie were serviceable but made no attempt at style or distinction. She thought there was an arrogance in this unconcern for the opinion of others. His speech was clipped and had an accent, maybe Scottish, she thought. He was lean. Perhaps he was one of those driven long-distance runners. Late fifties, she judged. She thought that for men at his stage of life something of a stomach was preferable, and reassuring. The offering of comfort was, in Deva's view, the principal opportunity for charm for men of that age. She decided that she did not much like this doctor who judged her coolly and did not hold her eye, and that she was unlikely to want to work with him.

He was saying now that his patient could remember events during the day but forgot everything each night. His sleep was atypical and profound. He was explaining the nature of trauma, which he said could be physical or psychological, or an interaction of both, and that the prospect of his patient regaining his memory depended on the skillful management of his environment, under his careful medical supervision.

Dr Elliot now turned from the window to give Deva an appraising look, as if to confirm for himself her amenability to his supervision. He turned away again before continuing. "He is not in any apparent distress. In fact, for the most part he seems content to live in a perpetual present. How much of this is his natural personality and how much a product of the brain damage is unclear. If you don't have a memory, you don't necessarily feel that you are missing one."

"I really don't understand how I could help," said Deva. "I don't see where an anthropologist comes in."

"Well, his companion will be the person best placed to pick up cultural cues. You would be the person closest to Harry day to day, and as his companion, the one who would first learn of any memories that might arise. I do expect some to arise. He is curious about the world, and you would be the person to answer his questions about it. Everything he says and asks will outline the shape of his consciousness. Everything you say to him will inhabit it. I will require detailed reports. This is subtle, responsible work."

Deva, feeling her assent was being demanded, stayed silent, and Mrs. Slater now spoke into this silence. "The thing is, we're not sure who he is. We don't know much about him. This is his house, but there are no family or friends in evidence. He's not obviously English, though his use of English is excellent."

"This is his house?" Deva was a little more interested.

"Yes," replied Dr Elliot. "You would meet him here. Not today. He presents well. You'll probably find him charming. The job will not be unpleasant, I think. His affect belies his fragility and the seriousness of the brain damage. Mrs. Slater is living here, so you would not be alone. And you would be reporting to me regularly, of course."

"I would have thought you needed a psychologist. Or a carer. This isn't my sort of work."

"It's quite well paid," said Mrs. Slater. "Technically, the patient will be your employer and, as you can see, he has resources. They are being held in trust, but any offer depends on his approval. You could meet him tomorrow."

"I'm not sure there's any point."

Mrs. Slater glanced at Dr Elliot and found encouragement there. "Well, Deva, we were unsure about saying anything at this stage, but the thing is we have reason to believe you already know this patient. So, we think your presence might be uniquely encouraging to his recovery. We believe you might even have spent the night with him just before his accident."

This astonishing statement hung in the air, while both Dr Elliot and Mrs. Slater studied Deva. At last, she said, "Did he drive a Porsche?"

"Yes," said Dr Elliot, "I understand he was driving a Porsche when he crashed."

Then this was the slightly disturbing lover who had somewhat surprised her by not contacting her again. The one who had accidentally dropped a strange photo. Or perhaps had deliberately placed the strange photo on her bedside table.

"So, you might already know more about him than we do," observed Dr Elliot carefully.

"Not really," said Deva.

"His name?" asked Mrs. Slater. "You remember what name he used?"

"Harry, I think. Is it Harry?"

"A second name?" pressed Mrs. Slater.

"I never knew. We only met once."

"You spent the night with him," asserted Dr Elliot. "Didn't you ask his full name? Didn't he leave a number? Some way to contact him?"

"No," replied Deva, not interested in further justifying herself. "I didn't ask. So, why don't you just tell me about him."

"Well, in fact we don't know all that much. And what we do know, we are not completely certain about. And, as a matter of good practice, we should not even tell you that."

"It's good practice not to tell me about the man I slept with?"

"It's better you know nothing. We do not want you to introduce memories to him, reliable or not. Everything must arise from him. He has to rebuild himself."

Deva considered this: it made a sort of sense. She said, "I liked him well enough. He was a bit sad. He was gentle with my daughter."

They were waiting for more, but Deva only offered, "So you think he wants to employ me?"

"Well, he doesn't remember you, of course," replied Mrs. Slater. "We'll know if he wants to employ you tomorrow."

"When he sees me, he might remember."

"Well, perhaps," said Mrs. Slater.

"He will not," said Dr Elliot. "And you should not hope that he will remember you, nor try to make him remember you. We have made his home calm. No TV, no phones, no news, and until now, no visitors. He cannot go out. We have seen what happens when his brain or emotions are excited. So, the rule is low key. Quiet talk. Subdued dress. We need a calm, familiar presence. Do you think you could manage that?"

"We were not that familiar. And last time wasn't that calm. I suppose I'll know when I meet him." As she said this, Deva understood that she did want to see Harry again. There was something unresolved about their first meeting, some grit in her shoe. Certainly, she had expected him to contact her again, but it was not exactly that. And it wasn't love; she was sure about that. It was an unsolved puzzle, an intensity she could not classify.

"It goes without saying that you will not resume as lovers," said Dr Elliot.

"Yet you said it," replied Deva.

Dr Elliot pursed his lips and Mrs. Slater stepped in. "When Harry wakes in the morning, each day is a new life to him. But sometimes he has the idea that someone else should be there in his bedroom—a woman—and he looks for her. It is some sort of expression of loneliness. He might imagine you are that person. There should be no confusion."

Deva restricted herself to a nod of concession.

"We will arrange for you to meet Harry tomorrow then," said Dr Elliot briskly. "Do you feel like you understand the assignment? Or should I go over it again?" Dr Elliot looked skeptical, like an artist who had been obliged to work with inferior materials.

Now Deva held Dr Elliot's eye, and in a carefully neutral tone, said, "Your patient is fragile and you are looking for someone to keep him company who will take your orders and not overstimulate him, while being alert to who he might be and to any signs of returning memory."

"Yes, essentially," conceded Dr Elliot. He turned from Deva to Mrs. Slater and said, "You'll manage things. Let them meet alone, but stay close by. And have Deva sign the papers." To Deva, he said, as he crossed the room to leave, "Medical confidentiality. And all that."

Honeyed light shone down on him. Sheets were smooth against his skin. The temperature was just right. His body felt well rested, muscles exactly as muscles should be, stretched, relaxed, and strong. This place of comfort into which he was being delivered was neither strange nor frightening, but he did not recognize anything about it. It raised questions of such extent that he declined to admit them, and he turned back towards unconsciousness. Harry did not know that he was Harry.

His life in dreams was waving small goodbyes, wishing him well. He would miss that life. Lines of waving hands honored him as hero as he passed between them, though all his heroic deeds were still ahead of him. He was his dream's envoy into consciousness and had been entrusted with a crucial task. They trusted him and he wanted to be worthy of their trust, though he also feared that they might have chosen him by mistake. Also, while he understood that everything depended on him, he did not know the exact nature of his task. They had forgotten to tell him. He tried to return to dream, but his existence there was fast receding. He was emerging into the spaciousness and light. Against this expanse, he closed his eyes. For one last time he looked back and understood that there was no longer a home for him in the unconscious. The waving hands were, in fact, expelling him.

He was in the center of a large bed in an airy room, faced by a wall of muted light, a big window covered by yellow curtains. On each side of the bed in a pleasing symmetry was a bedside table with a lamp, and beyond them, to left and right, walls lined with neat white doors and drawers, all closed. There was no clutter, no complication. He lifted the sheet and found there further symmetry: a youngish man, nicely formed and well displayed, naked and brown skinned against the ivory sheets. Himself. His penis flopped to one side, misaligned and comic. For now, he would stay still and only listen.

From his chest there was a steady thump. A pulse in his neck kept time with it. There was an intimate little noise from just behind his head, where the short hairs on his neck scraped the pillow. Then there was something outside the room, not close but within the same building—water rushing through a pipe. Beyond that was a low stew of sound, which did not identify itself until a horn was beeped: traffic.

His nose registered the cozy smell of his own stale perspiration. And from the far corner of the room, there was a sweet smell from behind a door that he understood to be a bathroom. He did not know how he knew this. The door behind him and to his right was the door to the world outside the room. He knew that too. So, he must have been here before. The idea of a before was slightly distressing. He could not find anything of himself in the before. His mind flickered into agitation and he stilled it. There was this now.

He resolved to stand, to go to the window, draw back the curtains, and look out upon the world. Standing was more demanding than he had imagined, but not difficult. It was a good feeling, to be upright. It gave you power. He stretched his arms and one met a wardrobe door, which he opened. There was an array of men's clothes, jackets hung, shirts folded, a rack of polished shoes. His, he supposed, though they did not seem quite so. As the door eased further open, he was reflected in a full-length mirror. He was a tallish man, even featured, thirties, neat dark hair, the shadow of a beard. He liked the look of himself well enough. His eyes were green with brown flecks, and he now looked into them in order to discover himself. Amiable, he thought, this man, though not easy to know.

He closed the wardrobe door and walked to the window. The white carpet pushed up between his toes. Delightful, that. He smiled at this tickle to his feet.

Behind the curtain was a wall of glass. He was high up in a

city. Across the street was a leaded roof belonging to a lower building. If he pressed himself forward against the window, he could just see the ground below, a sliver of clogged traffic moving slowly in a narrow street. There were red buses. "London" clicked in him. That he knew this and not his own name did not present itself as a contradiction.

In a window opposite and below, he caught a movement and then the eye of a woman—Japanese; he knew that too—looking up at where he stood pressed against the glass. Her expression was transfixed and amazed. Ah, of course, he was naked and pressed against the glass. He pulled back with an instinctive gesture of apology. The woman returned a faint smile and retreated into invisibility. He turned back to the room, half expecting to find a woman there, still asleep in the bed, and felt a slight disappointment not to do so.

From outside the room, shockingly close, came a brisk no-nonsense voice. A woman. Not young. It said, "Harry, are you awake?" Then, after a pause, "This is Mrs. Slater. Harry? I've put out your breakfast. You'll be taking it at the dining table. First you need to go to the bathroom. Read your notes on the mirror. Go to the bathroom, then come to breakfast."

He froze. The tone was informational and the central facts clearly laid out. She wanted him to know about the dining table. And breakfast. And that he was Harry. He had stepped onto a stage mid-play unarmed with any script. Could he speak? The woman's voice came again: "Can you hear me, Harry? This is Mrs. Slater. Harry, say *yes* if you understood what I said."

He took in the definite idea that he was Harry. That the speaker was a Mrs. Slater also impressed itself. "Yes," he said, discovering language. "Thank you. Thank you very much."

Outside Harry's room the hallway was glass-roofed and aglow with natural light. It opened on to a bigger space that was lighter still, two of its walls entirely glass, one of them a margin between the interior living space and a broad terrace beyond. After the terrace was a parapet and the sky. The space was open, stylish, inviting, and minimally furnished, so that he imagined flinging his body into its extent, dancing, flying even. Nestled by an inner wall was a long dining table, breakfast things arranged, a single place set in readiness. Magically, the foods on display all struck him as foods he was disposed to like. He looked around for Mrs. Slater, the agent of this miracle. No one. But of course, she would already know what he liked if he had started many days in this way, as the notes on his mirror had informed him. Harry told himself to accept this as fact.

He worked from one food to the next, pausing to top up his coffee. It was all delight. When sated, the windows claimed more of his attention. There was the sky, but also there were rooftops, intricately crafted peaks of cityscape. Also, in the far distance, he could make out a mist of green hills. All this was laid out in front of him as if he had commanded it.

"Do you need anything more, Harry? More toast?" came a voice next to him. Surprised, he turned to discover a compact woman with light gray hair and clothes mainly composed of darker grays. "I'm Mrs. Slater," the woman said, offering Harry a closed smile and a glance of keen intelligence.

"No, no. Nothing. Thank you, Mrs. Slater."

She piled up the dishes, not looking at Harry. He considered that this might be deference, then decided that it wasn't deference.

He said, "That was wonderful."

"Good. Now, you mustn't overdo things. Remember you've been ill."

"I think I feel well now."

"Did you read your list?"

"Yes. Is it always this wonderful here?"

"More or less always this wonderful."

"And this is mine? This house?"

"Everything is yours."

"It's lovely, isn't it?"

"Exceptional. I expect you'll want to explore it later. You usually do."

"Mrs. Slater, what happened to me?"

"You were in a car accident, Harry. You were unconscious for a long time. Then they brought you home."

"I feel well now. I slept well."

"Still, you need to be careful. Your brain is fragile. Not too much stimulation. No worrying. You probably can't remember very much, can you?"

"No."

"Do you know what you had for dinner last night?"

He thought, and felt an itch of discomfort that threatened to grow. He shook his head. His known life started in his dreams.

"Well," Mrs. Slater continued, "you mustn't worry."

"Did you know me before the accident, Mrs. Slater?"

"No. I was asked to take care of you after you came from the hospital."

Harry nodded agreeably. Mrs. Slater was disappointing. Opaque, he thought. Unlikely to dance in the light. He wondered how he might put her at her ease.

"I'll look in now and then," Mrs. Slater continued. "And if you need anything, pull the cord. I dare say you'll want to put your feet up on the couch after you've looked around." She was clearing the table, loading herself up, but hesitated in this work to add, "Later today, you'll probably have a visitor. An old friend. A woman. Deva."

"She's on my list."

"Exactly. She'll be your first visitor. If she comes. Dr Elliot will evaluate whether this is good for you."

At the terrace parapet, Harry looked down at the stop-start of the traffic in the street below. On each side of it, pedestrians were in unceasing motion. Wonderful, he thought, the way they avoided each other. The phrase, "Bustle of city streets," popped into his mind. Then, "Milling throng." Milling throng?

Harry thought about the nature of the breeze that brushed him, whether it could be said to be coming from somewhere or going towards somewhere, or just existing somewhere. It caught his shirt and billowed it. Wonderful that, to be part of the wind. He let his face feel it and inclined his head so that it whispered first in one ear, then the other. Cooking smells rose from restaurants in the street below. A plastic bag floated past him. A bird soared up there, using the currents of the air. Closer to him, a pigeon took flight with noisy, effortful flapping. He wondered what it was like to fly.

At last, he turned away from the view and walked back into the house, his attention now caught by the glossy expanse of wood floor, a sea of floor, that separated him from the far carpet, with its arrangement of couch and armchairs. He took off his shoes and tested the slipperiness. Not too slippery, but slippery enough. He slid a little, then ran a little and slid further, then took a real run to see if he could cross the entire floor in a single slide, and had nearly succeeded when he came up against an unsmiling Mrs. Slater. "Harry, you're convalescing from an injury. You need to rest."

"Yes," Harry conceded. "You're right. Of course, you're right. Where should I go?"

"Usually, you rest on the couch about now. Usually, you don't sleep."

"Right. Thank you. Perfect. Sorry, Mrs. Slater."

The couch was long and was bent around a coffee table. The covering was a soft, pale leather. He stretched out, closed his eyes. Very comfortable. Not hard, not soft. Words came to him from somewhere: "Not hard, not soft; not yours, not mine; a being in between…" There were more words, he was sure, but they did not come. He remembered his waking, just a couple of hours earlier, and that he had emerged into this life from a more serious world. There was a purpose that would reveal itself. He smiled. In a little while, he would explore the house. Later he would have a visitor.

After the troubling episode with the daffodils, John set about reassembling himself along the armature of routine. He thought about calling it a mini-stroke, but settled on "episode."

Each day he forced himself to stay in bed until six, even though sleep was impossible. He made his coffee and ran through a series of stretching exercises while listening to the news on National Public Radio. One day, after a week or so, he decisively threw out the vase of wilted daffodils, before sitting down as usual to granola and a second coffee. He checked the sports reports on his iPad, even though he had little interest in sport. He went through all the motions, but he had been opened up, and would not close.

At ten past seven, as usual, he set out on the eleven miles of winding roads that led to the gym in the college town, his BMW 5-series rattling from the years of New Hampshire frost heaves. He should have replaced the car by now; it was bad in snow and he could afford a new one. But he had become reluctant to change anything, fearing it might lead to a comprehensive unravelling of his settled life. At seven-thirty, he arrived at the gym, changed for a low-intensity workout and followed that with a ten-minute swim. At eight-fifteen he was sitting by the Jacuzzi chatting with the group of retired men with whom he chatted every morning. This slight community was the only reason he had looked up the daily sports results. He also went along with the group's liberal politics, keeping it bland. Several of the others had been college professors and liked to hear themselves talk, which suited John well enough. He was known as the resident expert on foreign affairs, and generally was deferred to on matters of fact. One had teased him with, "Come on, John. Come clean. You were really a spy, weren't you?" It was a sort of flattery, a running gag. "Hardly," he said. Then, forestalling the predictable, he added, "But of course I would say that." He had never been to their homes. They had not been to his. He guessed that they thought him an odd bird, and he settled for it.

John was still in his fifties when he bought the old farmhouse in New Hampshire, where he knew no one. It was an early retirement, not glorious. He dated from the Cold War era and there were those who thought that his generation was responsible for all more recent problems and were thus unqualified to address them. His early territory of Pakistan was a case in point. Superiors had weakly indicated Camden, Maine, for his retirement, where there was a nest of old hands messing about in boats, but John struck out on his own. They indicated too that he might be called upon from time to time, that his experience was too valuable to entirely lose, and they had occasionally tugged at that loose leash.

John had imagined that over the years new life might grow on his eight acres, that he might acquire some animals, receive visitors, be gentled. He had imagined, without admitting it, that if he waited long enough something might change in him, so that he would deserve love, and that love would therefore find him. Now he had been reminded that nothing had changed, and that it never would.

After leaving the gym, he sat in his car for a few minutes, managing the newly aching place in him that wanted to collapse inward. Then he turned to the solution he knew—blind habit— and drove into the centre of town, bought his customary *New York Times* at the general store, and went to read it across the way at Omar's Bookstore Café. He nearly always sat alone, preferably at this same table towards the back. Always drank a cappuccino with two shots. The girl baristas, a changing cast of students, often smiled at their regular, and this was the case today. It could be the warmest moment of his day, and John now tried to prolong it with some banter about her not needing to hurry since espresso had no *x* in it, but his humour was too dry for the girl so that she was unsure that it was humour, and her smile wavered.

Between his table and the door, there was the usual lively group that he thought of as the table of international women. Sometimes there were men, occasionally children, but women were the heart of it, mostly in their thirties. Some were actually foreign—today he identified a Brazilian, an Arab—probably Lebanese—a Latvian, a Turk, a French woman—while the others were travelled Americans with international tendencies. To his knowledge there were among this population, graduate students, young professors, a couple of writers, a painter, a psychotherapist, and an architect. They were always animated, even raucous, and John viewed them as the town's nexus of human warmth. They would be surprised to know how closely he had observed them, but now they seemed to be observing him, and he wondered if their laughter might be at his expense, the older man with his old-fashioned newspaper, who never went beyond hello. Perhaps they noticed something new about him, some outer sign of his inner disorder. Or it could be that the one he had talked to on the phone had told the others, in spite of the promise of confidentiality.

That woman, not here today, worked for an outfit called, You Must Remember This, which helped old people write memoirs that were bound into a book for posterity, or at least for the grandchildren. Her cards were tucked into the café's bulletin board. The impulse to call had followed his dismissal of the notion to seek out a psychotherapist, which would be professionally unacceptable. There had been instead the vague idea of pouring out his life to an attractive, sympathetic woman who would then deliver him one of their red-bound books that only he would read before his death. It was, he acknowledged, the impulse to confess, perhaps to have the chance to be fully known. After the call, he gave up the idea. This was not because of the shockingly high cost, but because he thought that the woman might not be sympathetic. She might be disgusted, and refuse to write his story, delivering not absolution or validation, but their opposites. Now someone at the table, the Latvian, accidentally met his eye and gave him a little wave, regular to regular. They were nice women.

It was ten-thirty. Time to head home. To pick up milk and coffee filters at the general store, and head back. He knew what he was eating for lunch and when—twelve-thirty. He knew what he would have for dinner at seven. He would not talk to anyone until the next morning at the gym.

"John!" The voice came from the driver of a car in the café's disabled spot. Gwen earned her spot fairly through spinal sclerosis. She was his old supervisor, over eighty now, but still more in the loop than him. If the international women in the café had ever noticed him with anyone else, it would have been Gwen, who occasionally visited to chew over old times, and to monitor him. Today was not on their schedule.

"Hello, Gwen. Did we plan something?"

"No. Excuse me not getting out, John. Not worth the trouble, really. Look, John, about the memoir thing. Don't. Technically, you can't. So, just don't."

"I wasn't planning to." He didn't bother to ask how she knew.

"Good. That's all right then." Gwen gave a sigh of exasperation, and turned her long eyes to appraise him. "Look, John, I know they treated you badly. They know it too. They want to make it up to you. Have faith."

"That's all? Faith?"

"That's all. Many miles for few words. Very good, I'll be off. I'm a danger on the roads these days. Sooner or later, I'll kill someone. We're on for next Thursday, aren't we?"

"Right. See you then." He watched her back out, feeling fingers moving in a wound.

The man stood up from the couch and walked towards Deva, smiling, offering his hand, a pre-existing grace wired in. He was slim, neat, and dressed casually, but expensively. Understated, Deva thought. She took the hand, and they stayed like that, in touch, until Mrs. Slater clattered the tea things. Deva thought she remembered, and liked, the scent of him.

"I'm Deva."

"I know. I'm Harry, I'm told."

"You know me?" Deva took a step back and smiled, as if the full sight of her—green blouse, tight white skirt, green heels, hair piled, earrings, necklace, bangles, and rings adorning—would serve for more powerful reminding.

Harry shook his head. "Sorry. Only that Mrs. Slater said you were coming and I wrote it down. But I know you are my friend."

"We were new friends, really."

"How did we know each other?"

"I've been told not to tell you. I'm not supposed to tell you anything I know about you. Which, actually, isn't that much."

Harry considered this. "They think I shouldn't know about myself?"

"They think it might confuse you. You'd have my memories instead of yours. False memories." She made a face, as if this was officious nonsense.

The door to Mrs. Slater's quarters closed shut and they both turned their heads towards it, then back towards each other, neither one finding it necessary to mention that they were now alone.

"Yes, but…" started Harry at last when his eyes were settled back on Deva's. "Well, never mind. There's tea. Shall we?"

They walked over to the couch and sat, synchronized, as if rehearsed. Harry continued. "Did they say you shouldn't tell me about yourself as well?"

Deva considered. "No, I don't think that was mentioned."

"Good. Then we'll have something to talk about. I want to know everything."

"Okay. I'm from Brazil originally. I have a daughter. Nadia. I'm a mother. That's the first thing. And I'm a singer in a Brazilian nightclub. Here, in London. You were a customer. Oh, you see, now I've told you something. What do you think? I don't like Dr Elliot's rules. Did that feel too confusing?"

Harry laughed. "No, I don't feel confused. It's good. I knew beautiful Deva while she was singing in a Brazilian nightclub. I had a good life. And, you know, tomorrow you can tell me again."

"Also," said Deva, "I do research at a university. As an anthropologist. You know what that is?"

"You study human cultures."

"Sorry, Harry. But…how is it that you know some things but can't remember other things?"

"I don't know. I don't know where things come from." He faltered, then rallied. "So, they want you to study me? I'm an interesting example, perhaps?"

"They want me to keep you company. That's what they told me. To help you make your new life. And maybe you'll recover some memories. You can ask me anything about the world, just not about yourself."

"So, Deva…that's a Brazilian name?"

"D-e-v-a. Not D-i-v-a. I've never met another one. I think my mother made it up."

"Of course. The one and only Deva. Do I still seem like the same person?"

Deva studied him. "Honestly, Harry, I'm surprised. Yes… but you seem more relaxed now. Even though you've been through so much. You smile more. Your eyes seem clearer. I remember you said you liked a particular song of mine. It was the saddest song I ever sing. A very, very sad song. Though you couldn't understand a word—it was in Portuguese."

Harry was thoughtful for a moment. "You know, I don't have any family. It's one of the things I've written down. They must have told me."

"And when I just mentioned sadness, you thought of that?"

"Yes. Is that interesting?"

"You did tell me your parents were dead. If you already know you have no family, I suppose I can say it."

Harry started to ask a question, then stopped, and said, "Now you're sad. Don't you have family either?"

"Oh, I do. I have my daughter, Nadia. We're very happy."

Harry studied Deva, then turned away to pour tea, then returned his gaze to her, then smiled. "Deva, you're like the spring. You're like when flowers break through the snow."

Deva sat back. "What? Where did that come from?"

"I don't know."

Deva shook her head, and laughed. "You're supposed to be brain damaged, not charming." She thought for a moment. "You're not entirely wrong. I did live through a winter."

When conversation dwindled, they put down their empty cups and Harry closed his eyes, leaning back into the couch.

"I've tired you," said Deva. "I don't know how I ended up talking so much."

"I like to listen to you."

"Well, anyway, that's me. Born in Brazil. Never knew my father. Studied in America, and now here. Picked up a daughter along the way. Did you really want to know all that?"

"I did. I don't know why. And where would you say I'm from, Deva? As an anthropologist."

"From your accent, you're from here, London. And this is your home, right? So, here."

"It seems so."

"Obviously, from your looks, some of your family was originally from somewhere else. But Londoners come from everywhere these days, most of them mixed up places. Speaking as an anthropologist, there's something else, but I can't place it. Some other cultural influence. For an Englishman, you're a bit too…graceful. And you don't shake hands exactly the way they do. You shake hands more like you're feeling something through your fingertips."

"Brazilian like you? We're a bit alike? Skin. Eyes."

"Well, we do both have green eyes. But you don't seem to speak Portuguese. And whatever the cultural influence is in you, it isn't Brazilian. I know Brazilian."

Mrs. Slater appeared in front of them, and they stopped talking to take notice of her. She bent over to put the tea things back onto a tray, saying as she did, "Dr Elliot said twenty minutes. It's already much more. Harry, you have to let Deva go now. You need to rest. And, Deva, Dr Elliot wants to see you."

Deva stood up on the green high heels, smoothed down her skirt, and addressed herself exclusively to Harry. "So, do you want me?"

"Do I want you?"

"Do you want me to keep you company. To work for you."

"Of course. Do you want to come?"

"Yes."

"You know, Deva, I will not remember any of this next time we meet. Almost certainly. Will that be annoying?"

"Well, maybe you will remember something. Anyway, I don't think you'll be annoying. You're…pleasant."

"Unburdened by memory?" Harry stopped to consider his own words, then asked, "Is that something the English say about memory—*unburdened*?"

Deva looked towards Mrs. Slater. "You should ask someone English."

"Mrs. Slater?" Harry enquired. She was waiting, holding the tray.

"I've heard *burdened*."

"Burdened by memory. Thank you. Good. Therefore, unburdened by the loss of it? Now, would you tell the doctor that I want Deva to visit, and that she wants to visit? And that she has a daughter, Nadia, to look after, so we must pay her double."

"It doesn't work like that, Harry."

"But didn't you say everything here belongs to me? That I pay? That I would pay Deva?"

"Yes…"

"So…I think, that's good."

As they walked away together, Mrs. Slater said to Deva, "You overstimulated him. And Dr Elliot told you to dress simply… You understand, don't you, that by tomorrow he will have forgotten everything he said?"

"Yes, yes," said Deva. "But we will remember, won't we?"

Harry went to his bathroom and amended the notes to his future self, adding: *Deva is my friend. I trust her.*

When Deva introduced herself each morning, Harry always said that he already knew of her, and that she was his friend and that he trusted her. Each day he lit up with delight at the sight of her, and Deva dressed for that moment, more Latin, more color, more skin, more jewelry. She was Harry's daily miracle, and she treasured his reaction. Each day, she reminded Harry of how they met and confirmed that she knew nothing of his life before his accident, except for this one meeting. Then he would ask about it, and she would tell him about the Miranda, instinctively omitting that they had spent the night together, and had made love. There was nothing like that now.

After a week or two of this, when Mrs. Slater's vigilance was eroded by the repetition, and after the morning's coffee things were removed, Deva sat next to Harry on the couch and set before him on the expanse of emptied coffee table the photo he had left at her flat. She said nothing.

Harry looked closely at the photo, then looked again, while Deva studied him. At last, he said, "What is it?"

She said, "I don't know. I think it's your photo. I found it after we first met. Perhaps you dropped it by accident." Deva was anxious about its effect. She had not told Dr Elliot about the photo. She sensed that it would be against the rules, and that there was something wrong with the rules. It was just between her and Harry.

He looked at it again, and said, "It could be mine." Then, "Don't you think?"

"I do think," said Deva. "Probably, you left it by accident. It's the only clue I have from before. Does it seem familiar?"

Harry turned back to the photo, then asked, "Who is the man? Do you know?" Deva shook her head, but he was not looking at her. He said, "This man is in love with the daffodil." Then, "He's stiff. Look how he's bending over. Quite old, I think. He's stiff. Maybe he's in pain. And he's facing away from the camera. He's alone. He looks vulnerable. Undefended." He touched the photo lightly with his fingertips, running them over the mass of daffodils amongst which the man was bending. Deva noticed the neatness of Harry's nails.

Each subsequent day, the photo aroused in Harry the same intense interest in this window on to his life before. The background was the landscape behind a rural house. There was rough grass rising up a hill, some exposed rock, patches of snow in the shadows, the remains of an old drystone wall, and surrounding that on all sides, was forest, a mixture of bare deciduous trees and conifers. On its left margin, out of focus in the poorly framed photo, was the corner of a white house. It was springtime and part of the dull grassy area had been overtaken by the luminous daffodils, amongst which the man was bending. All that could be seen of him were khaki trousers, a beige cardigan hanging open, and gray hair cut to stubble.

Deva said, on Harry's most recent time of asking, "I don't know who he is. We've been trying to find out. You've been asking me questions about him every day for three weeks now. I've been going to the British Library, doing research for you. I can tell you what we've found out so far."

"Yes. Good."

"Well, you've asked me a lot about daffodils, and what they mean. You are interested in who the man is, of course, and why you had his photo. You asked about the trees, and where in the world looks like that. And where people wear clothes like that. Specifically, you've been interested in cardigans. Oh, and you keep asking me about happiness. Something about looking at a photo of this man's back makes you ask about happiness. What does it mean, and so on. It's a big question."

Harry smiled. "Sorry." Once again, he pored over the photo. "But I can see why I ask… It's because the man is happy in this photo. At this moment. Yet he's not happy. It's complicated—I can feel it. It's about happiness. That must be why I asked."

"How can you know all that from looking at a photo of the back of someone's head?"

"I don't know... I can. He's very still, isn't he?"

"It seems so."

"He's stopped doing what he was doing and he's still."

"And that's happiness?"

"Perhaps. He's still. He's lost in looking into the particular flower he's holding. You see?"

"How are you so sure?"

Harry shook his head, as if disturbed by the question. "I don't know." He bent closer to the photo to search for explanation. "Look, he was going to cut the flower—you can just see the glint of something, knife, or scissors, in his right hand—but he's stopped. Something stopped him. He was lost in thought and then became lost in the flower. That's it. He was unhappy before and will be unhappy again but at this moment, he's happy. And he's defenseless. Someone is watching from behind him, taking this picture, but he's not aware of it. His back...if I go into his back..."

"Don't try too hard, Harry. Go easy on your brain."

Harry asked, the thought freshly occurring to him, "Is there something special about daffodils?"

"Oh, Harry, you ask me something like that nearly every day. I'll summarize what I've learned from my research, okay? I'm starting to feel a lot like a daffodil myself, so you'll learn about me too. Anyway, daffodils originally come from Iberia—Spain, Portugal—though before either one of those was invented. My family came from Portugal, by the way. At least, part of it did. Daffodils spread around the world from there, moving east by land, north African, Italy, Greece, Turkey, and across Asia all the way to Japan. And you know how they managed to move so far?" Deva waited until Harry looked at her. "Because they were beautiful and people loved them. People loved them and carried them with them and nurtured them and selected the shapes and colors they liked. The ancient Greeks cultivated them, so did the Romans. There's the Greek myth about daffodils, about Narcissus anyway."

"Narcissism? Vanity?"

"Yes. Exactly. Of course, you know the word. Your vocabulary is... Do you know the story too?"

"Harry smiled, shook his head. "I want you to tell me."

"Okay. So...anyway. Narcissus was the beautiful boy who died because he loved his own reflection in a pond too much. His punishment. Supposedly, he was turned into the flower when he died. The daffodil's proper name is *Narcissus pseudo-narcissus.*"

"And you're like that?"

"Vain? Surely, you've noticed? Look at me. I'm decorated." She picked at the elaborate necklace that filled the space between neck and breasts, tugged at a long earring, fluttered a hand to show its rings.

"I've noticed. You're adorned."

"Adorned... Yes, exactly. You have the words. But I meant mainly that daffodils are like me because we come from the same place, and my family also moved around the world because of love. Because of their beauty, really, I suppose. At least the women. One of my great-grandmothers was brought from India by a man who fell in love with her. Another came from Cape Verde in Africa for the same reason. And my grandmother was taken to Brazil by a Portuguese man. So, you see, beauty is love, is destiny. And I only exist because of beauty. A man could not resist my beautiful mother."

Harry was studying the photo again. "So, for daffodils, beauty is their destiny."

"Ah, Harry, you have to be careful! There's another story for daffodils. Quite interesting. That story is that they were not named because of a beautiful boy at all, but because they are dangerous. The first letters of narcissus are the same as for narcotic. Something that makes you numb. Same origins. You know, like opium."

"Opium? Yes." Harry looked searchingly at Deva, then

looked inwardly for something in himself, and not finding it, shook his head, saying, "A narcotic. That's...not so good. Is it?"

Deva studied Harry, then put her hand on his arm until she saw the struggle fall from his face. "Well, anyway," she continued, "daffodils contain a neurotoxin. If you eat enough daffodil bulbs, they'll kill you. Sometimes people have made a fatal mistake by confusing them with onions. In smaller doses they've been used for lots of medicines—potency, wounds, baldness. There's much more I could tell you, if you want me to carry on. You've turned me into an expert. Do you know the number one favorite poem of the English is about daffodils, and it's the national flower of Wales? Though it's obvious it's from somewhere warmer and more passionate. Look at them. That shameless color."

Harry peered back into the photo, and said, "You wouldn't imagine they were poisonous."

"They're very clever, don't you think? Humans love them and animals fear them. Beautiful and deadly." She flashed her eyes at Harry.

At the British Library, Deva also studied memory. She read that memory was imagination by another name, the past restaged and revised each time it was recalled. It was imprinted with all the whorls and quirks of the imaginer's brain, all the rememberer's history, along with all the imprints of her forebears, so that a memory could be said to be as much about the rememberer as the thing remembered. It therefore occurred to Deva, while sitting at her desk of pale wood, that it said so much about her that her earliest memory was of a deft, slender woman in a long blue skirt and pure white blouse who hardly seemed to touch the ground: her young mother at the kitchen sink, her back to her.

At the British Library, done with researching the anthropology of daffodils and cardigans, the geographical distribution of trees, the nature of happiness, and her own first name, Deva read the books on memory, concerned by Harry's loss of one, and now considering her own. It seemed obvious when she thought of it, that, given the brain's soft, slippery character that this must be the way it worked. There was nothing stored, nothing durable and crisp to be pulled intact from angular filing cabinets, only memories re-made according to present purpose, each time revised, and so always moving stepwise further from objective truth. We were our own dupes, forever convinced that the way we pictured things was the way they were, always mistaking memory for knowledge.

In memory, the mother is young and lovely. She turns to Deva and smiles. Deva is sitting at a table, at a high chair perhaps, a small child. The mother's smile is loving and peaceful, in memory, as she works gracefully and efficiently. There was this impression more than there was a face. There is just the two of them, and they were complete, just as Deva and Nadia were now complete, no man to dilute them. It is a kitchen table, and the sink her mother works at is stone. Deva felt sure of these details, though knowing them to be suspect. There is a hotplate fueled by a gas cylinder. The table is topped with white enamel with indented black shapes where the enamel has been chipped, which are of great interest to little Deva. They are of modest means, the furnishings worn and cheap. Her mother is young, beautiful, and calm. Food is coming. Deva is loved, and secure in love. There is no hint of any other presence, no father, no grandparents, no other children; there is simplicity. Deva felt she was happy then, though perhaps, even at that age, she was worried for her mother. There is the sense that the mother might need the help of the child, that the child might be stronger than the parent. Memory does not bother with labels, so that Deva was not sure exactly where they were, somewhere in Brazil, Rio perhaps. If she could, Deva would ask a brother or sister, but she had none. Perhaps a distant uncle or aunt might still know, but they were no longer in touch. There was no father to ask; she had never known one.

What Deva's mother had said about her father was this: that he was a very nice man, kind, charming, and handsome, an American, a Norte Americano; that he had been visiting their country to help the poor people there; that his name was Jim; that by the time her mother had known she was pregnant—she was only sixteen—they had already lost contact, so that he had never known of Deva; and that when she had tried to contact him, no one would tell her how. Also, Deva's mother said, that if he, Jim, had known he had a daughter as lovely as Deva, he certainly would have wanted to be her father and would have loved her. But, she conceded, she had not searched too hard or long, because she thought Jim might have another family in America, and she did not want to embarrass him, or herself, and, anyway, she liked Deva being entirely in her care. She said, "You are all mine, Deva. I am so lucky. My Deva!"

Deva used similar words with Nadia, who had enquired more than once why Deva did not settle with just one man to be a husband, and a father. Deva did not know for sure whether in this seeming repetition of her mother's words, the past had begat the present, or the present was conjuring the past. Such were the duplicities of memory. Her mother had said that Deva was conceived in love, and that the only sad thing about it was that Jim had been cheated out of the pleasure of knowing his wonderful daughter. Poor warm, kind, handsome Jim. She said she had named Deva after him, but Deva could make no sense of this.

There was this question, and others, that Deva would have asked her mother if, when she was older, her mother had still been alive. Instead, there had been her cancer, which, it had sometimes seemed to Deva, her mother had failed to adequately resist. There dwelled deep within Deva an anger at this that she knew to be unjust. The anger, she both understood and yet resisted understanding, had more to do with her own guilt.

But there had been this in her mother, a lightness of touch, a disinclination to fight, as if all the world was nature and she was naturally part of it. In this view, resistance would be close to hubris. Her cancer, in Deva's memory, came quickly, and quickly led her to lie still, making her presence faint, so that Deva's noise could no longer reach her. When her mother had achieved an almost complete separation, the cancer had transported her to death. It seemed to Deva, in memory, that her mother had been less happy when Deva was thirteen than when she was aged three. Or, perhaps, it was herself who had been less happy. She wondered now, sitting at her wide desk of golden wood at the British Library, whether this unhappiness was why her mother had surrendered life. She wondered whether it had been because of what she, Deva, had done to her mother when she was thirteen. And she thought that it was a terrible thing about the mind that it could create awful memories in support of awful ideas. She felt the resistance in her against such memories, and the consolidating of the same memories under the pressure of this resistance.

Deva led herself back to the small child at the kitchen table, three, maybe four, and watched her mother through those young eyes. The mother was still a girl herself really, perhaps only nineteen. Deva let herself dwell in her mother's grace, her mother's story of Deva's good father mislaid, and the chipped shape on the enamel table that resembled a black sheep. Then, newly apprised of the suspect nature of her memories, that the impression of her mother's vulnerability might, after all, have come from a later understanding, more likely derived from an older Deva and transplanted back, since, at three, what separate definition could there have been to imprint, any more than there was a distinction in the air they breathed? And Deva might, she reluctantly conceded, have exaggerated her mother's disinclination to resist death to release herself from the idea that Deva had herself hastened it. It was suspicious, she thought, that each time she summoned memory, there was a little more tragedy in her mother's smile.

After three weeks of studying the photo, a name arose in Harry: John Bradley. As was his habit, he had been concentrating on the photo with his intense attention on the back of the man bending over daffodils. Then the name arrived out of nowhere, out of a trance, intact, no further information attached, leaving Harry surprised, and inexplicably distressed. Deva asked if it was the man's name and Harry replied, "I think it must be." She held his hands and enquired gently as to feelings, trying to settle him, but he could not explain the distress except to say that it was like a passing storm, something awful moving through him, but not really of him. It would not last, he assured Deva, and it did not.

The following morning, in a definitive break from all that had gone before, Harry could still recall the name, John Bradley, and with it, the previous day, so that Harry's accumulation of a new history started then.

Deva's diligent research at the British Library into the photo's vegetation, the particular mixture of deciduous trees and conifers in the background forest, narrowed things down to an inland region of New England in America, and within that limited ambit, there was only one John Bradley to be found, a man living in the countryside of New Hampshire, close to a college town.

Harry's new ability to make memories was a breakthrough that Deva could not keep from Dr Elliot. Nor did she try to conceal the photo that prompted it, nor the name of the man whose identification seemed to have opened the door in Harry's mind. This door, though, admitted only new memories, not the old ones from before.

"Let's go over this again," said Dr Elliot. "What was he like, exactly, when he remembered the name?"

"Distressed. Surprised. A bit disoriented. He'd been deep in concentration. It didn't last long. He soon regained his balance. But he's still very interested in this man. He's convinced that he must hold the key to something. The past? Now it's all he thinks about."

"And what's your considered opinion, Deva? Do you think contact with this man might do him good? Or would it just upset him?"

"You really want my opinion?"

"Yes, your opinion. An opinion is not a decision."

"I think if Harry wants us to find this man, we should find him."

"And you say you've already located him? Just from the name?"

"I think so."

"Impressive. Well, I've consulted my colleagues and on balance we think we might move cautiously in that direction. I want you to contact the man and tell him about your friend Harry. You can say that you are not sure about Harry's name, or much else about him. Find out if he knows him and whether he's willing to help. Report back to me."

"And if he's not willing to help? Or unsure?"

"Well, then we might consider sending you to America to persuade him."

"That would be Harry's decision, wouldn't it? His expense."

"I'd see it as part of his treatment. If this man can help restore Harry's memory, we have to explore it. And don't you think Harry would want you to go? At any expense?"

"Probably. Yes, I'm sure he would."

In Omar's Bookstore Café, a Frenchwoman at the table of lively international women was regarding John as he took his coffee from the barista. She said, "He comes in every day, but he never says hello to us."

To which, the Brazilian, replied, "He said hello to me once. He speaks some Portuguese."

"Who reads a paper newspaper these days?" said the Indian.

"I don't think he's a professor." The American. "He must have been handsome when he was younger."

"He's still handsome," said the Indian.

"Attractive older man seeks foreign woman for erotic adventures. You're interested?" The American again.

"Don't discount, is all I'm saying. No ageism," replied the Indian.

They all watched now, with their separate thoughts, while John carried his coffee to a far table up against the back wall of the café. Just as he set about unfolding his *New York Times*, an old lady with a stick intruded on their view stumping her way towards him. She was bent and lame, but moved with such assertive purpose that a path opened up before her.

"There's your competition," said the Frenchwoman.

"Or his mother," said the Peruvian.

Gwen took a moment to arrange herself on the chair opposite John before fixing him with her long eyes, the part of her least touched by ruin.

"You're well, John?"

"Yes. Generally. I did have a minor episode."

"Meaning?"

"I lost consciousness. Briefly. Had flashbacks. It was cold. I was outside bending over my garden. I'd forgotten to put on a hat."

"Are you going soft, John? What sort of flashbacks?"

"A variety. Can I get you a coffee, Gwen?"

"No, never mind. What sort of flashbacks?"

"One was an explosion."

"Africa? Afghanistan?"

"Just an explosion."

Gwen considered this, and him. "You want me to tell anyone?"

"No. It was just a distant explosion. I'm retired."

"You know that doesn't really happen. I'm eighty-three and here I am. We don't really want it, do we? John, you're in a rut. You're living among bumpkins. You need a trip."

"I took a trip."

"And you were used. I'm sorry."

"You have something in mind, I take it."

"London. Someone wants to make amends. A few people still remember us. We can't refuse, can we? Your last visit to Pakistan. The personal one to see your old friend?"

John nodded.

"There was the drone strike that killed the Taliban leader."

"My friend's son."

"The very successful drone strike. The very important and very successful drone strike that pleased everyone." Gwen fixed him with a look that dared him to contradict her.

"That also killed his father," he said. "My friend."

"Not intended. You know the difficulties. Anyway, it's brought you back. Brought you back into favor."

"And I should be pleased?"

"Yes. Your friend had a younger son. He had three sons. But only the younger one is of interest."

"Are the others dead?"

"Well, yes. The youngest one was also in Pakistan at the time of the strike. Then he went underground. We know he was in Lebanon. He visited America. Then went back to London. We assume he was radicalized and recruited. We assume he was on a terrorist mission. But we don't know what it was."

"Was?"

"Well, there was a fuck up. The British were tasked with surveillance and bringing him in. It seems there was a car chase and he crashed."

"Killed?"

"No. Brain damage. He's lost his memory."

"Convenient."

"Yes, suspicious. But the Brits can't find out what he was up to."

"And they want my help?"

"I'll get to that. Do you remember the son?"

"There were sons in the background during my time. Young, but able enough to work for us. It was thirty years ago, remember. They were our allies then. Against the Soviets. When I visited Pakistan last year, it was just a social call. For old times' sake. But you know that. How old is this youngest son now?"

"Mid-thirties. And don't play naïve, John."

"Then he was a small child when I worked there. He would have still been with the women. I wouldn't have known him. Where is he now?"

"In British care. They are waiting for his memory to return."

"And my role?"

"Well, you know the family. You understand his background. You could be useful."

"I'm not an interrogator. You know, I think I might have met him once. The whole family visited New York years after the war and I met them at a restaurant. Just social. There were a lot of them, but a boy was with them. Quiet and very polite, as I recall. He didn't really make an impression. His older sister was much noisier. He went to a fancy English school, I think. Seemed very English. I'm not sure I was even told his name. Could that be the one?"

"Possibly. As I understand it, he claims not to know who he is or even what country he's from. Nothing at all. But this is where it becomes interesting, John. You can expect a personal invitation to visit him. The beauty of it is that the invitation is not from us and not from the British. It comes through the Brazilian woman who is his carer. She's not a professional. She's in the dark about everything. All she knows is that he's been injured and that he's rich. She's doesn't even know he's under surveillance. But, amazingly, she found you. And she's got the idea that you must be a friend who could help him. Needless to say, the powers-that-be love this. You'll be right inside the house. Innocently invited."

"How did she find me?"

'Through an old-fashioned photograph, apparently. Of you at your farmhouse."

"No one comes there."

"Well, someone did. Maybe he did."

"Came to my house?"

"Well, he's the obvious candidate. It was his photo. Anyway, when the Brazilian woman contacts you, be confused and reluctant before you finally agree to go to London. If possible, get her over here first to persuade you. We want eyes on her."

"I haven't agreed."

"But you will. You're going to seed doing nothing. Of course you're going to agree. I'm told the Brazilian woman is very attractive, by the way. Beautiful and intelligent. A nightclub singer. They say you'll like her."

"How could they possibly know? Or care."

"Yes, that was strangely personal. You can confirm tomorrow. Walk me out, John."

They stood. John took Gwen's arm and she shook him off, saying, "Just follow me." She launched herself towards the exit at a rapid hobble that prompted someone to hurry to open the door for them to exit unimpeded.

"Hot date," commented the Brazilian woman, *sotto voce*, as they passed, precipitating the table of lively foreign women into waves of suppressed laughter.

"She couldn't even wait for her coffee," said the French-woman.

Nearly every day Harry had asked Deva for more about how they first met, and finally she started telling him. She did not care that Dr Elliot had forbidden such stories. She thought that she now knew better what might soothe Harry and unfurl his mind. What she had told Harry of their meeting at the Miranda had been a little different at each telling, but now that Harry's ability to remember new things had returned there could only be a single version, though one always subject to embellishment.

The story of Deva's first meeting with Harry began just after she had finished her final set at the Miranda on an upbeat encore. She was on her way to check that Nadia was still asleep on the couch in the upstairs office, when Ricardo, the manager, caught her elbow. "I can't," she said. "I have to get Nadia home."

"Ah, what will I do?"

"My guess? Fuck a waitress." She didn't care.

"Anyway, it's not that," said Ricardo. "One of your admirers wants to thank you. He loves your singing."

"My singing?"

"Just say hello. Just take a minute." Which Deva took to mean that Ricardo had already pocketed a tip.

"Old and fat?"

"No, in fact young and handsome."

"Okay. Maximum five minutes."

"On the right. In a booth on his own. Patricia's his waitress."

The smile with which Deva approached the booth was her deliberately tired smile, making an early case for the later offering of regrets. The man stood and looked at her, not finding words, not offering his hand. Shy, she thought.

Perhaps in awe. She tried to place him. Brownish but with a complexion pale enough for the pink in his cheeks to show through. Probably not European. Maybe south European. She tried Arab: the expensive, unimaginative suit, an awkwardness with women. Persian? Could be. Or Asian—an international Indian perhaps but, no, probably not dark enough, not smiling enough. More likely he was one of those wildly cosmopolitan mixtures that were all the rage in London now, and which helped her feel at home. A French-Lebanese mother and a Japanese-Indian father, that sort of thing. The new English.

She said, "I was told you want to meet me."

"Yes." Still he stared at her. "Yes, your singing. Wonderful. I mean, it moved me. Please, will you sit?"

Deva accepted, sitting without relaxing. He did seem in some sort of emotional state. She took in the face again and felt that she had seen it somewhere before in a context that did not connect. "I'm sorry. I can't stay long," she said. "I have to take my daughter home."

"You have a daughter?"

"You sound surprised. Yes, my little girl. My Nadia. She's asleep upstairs."

"How old is she?"

"Just seven."

"But you can stay for a quick drink?" he said. "You must be thirsty. It was hot under those lights."

London accent, she thought. Deva turned to catch Patricia and ordered for herself. "Some water please, Patricia. Still."

"We're not good customers for the bar, are we?" he observed, indicating his own Perrier.

Moslem? she wondered.

He continued. "That music…the sad song that nobody danced to. It was beautiful."

"The fado? Of course." When he remained silent, she continued. "You understand what it means, fado?"

He shook his head. "Not exactly."

So, Deva thought, no Brazilian roots, then, or Portuguese, or anything like. Probably a first timer at the Miranda. She said, "It means destiny. The words come from the suffering of Portugal's poor. That one was about the death of a loved one. About accepting loneliness. Always about death and loneliness." She laughed. "But I'm pleased you liked it."

"Liked?" He stumbled. "It spoke to me. Even though I didn't understand a word, I knew it was poetry."

Deva considered this, nodded, then took her glass of water from Patricia. He was a little more interesting now. The expensive suit actually did not fit him well. And as he talked, he had loosened his tie without thinking, as if not used to it. She said, "Fado speaks to everyone who has known sadness."

He assented with a slight movement of his head, but offered no elaboration, finally asking, "Excuse me, but weren't you crying when you sang?"

"It's a tragic song."

"But your tears were real. I nearly cried too." For a moment he bowed his head.

Which means he did cry, Deva thought, but said, "You know, you haven't told me your name."

"Oh, Harry." He said it, then caught himself, then resolved something before repeating, "Harry."

Deva saw the moment, but let it pass. He could call himself whatever he liked. She said, "You're from here?"

He nodded. "Yes. London. I already know you're from Brazil. It's posted on the board outside. Brazil, Portugal, America."

"Isn't Brazil America?"

"Of course, but you know what I mean. The US."

"That was on the board?"

"I think so."

"I didn't know that. Do I have an accent?"

He shrugged. "Maybe a bit."

There was something complicated about him. Deva blurted, "Do I already know you from somewhere?"

Harry looked up. "It's my first time here. I came by chance."

Deva thought that something in this was not true, and that he was not a good liar. She did not care.

Harry returned the conversation to its earlier course: "I was wondering if you'd lost someone yourself?"

She said, "There was my mother when I was a child," though this was not the first loss that came to mind.

"But you still have your father?"

She laughed. "Hardly." He waited and Deva reluctantly obliged. "I never knew my father. He was just a story my mother told me. There was a time when I looked for him. Then I stopped." Harry nodded gravely, and she added, "You don't miss what you never had."

Deva felt that she was confiding too much, that her nature was too open. She asked, "And you? Your parents live here in London too?"

"No, I lost my parents." He paused before adding, "An accident."

Deva broke the silence that followed with, "I'm sorry. It's hard to lose a parent. For my mother it was cancer. But that was a long time ago."

"Not so long for me," he said.

Deva felt a deadweight fall between them, so that she touched the back of his hand lightly with her own, the minimum of comfort. She said, "I have to go." Lonely and sad men with dubious stories were a professional hazard.

Harry removed his hand and leaned back in the booth, giving her an appraising look that she could not exactly read. Then something clicked for her: "I think I know where I've seen you," she said. "Aren't you a friend of Bill's?"

"Bill? No, I don't think so."

It was a code for Alcoholics Anonymous, and now Deva did not know how to proceed. If he wanted to remain anonymous, he had the right. Still, she was almost certain that she had seen him sitting at the back of the Bloomsbury meeting. Then there was the supporting evidence of his Perrier. "Sorry," she said. "Maybe the university? Did you study here?"

"I did."

"What did you study?"

"Poetry. I studied poetry."

"Honestly? Well, that explains it. The fado. You're a poet."

He shook his head. "It's gone now."

"Gone where?"

"Away. I have to take care of the family business." Before Deva could decide whether or not she wanted to hear more about this, he added with finality, "Import, export," and looked down towards the tabletop.

"Come on," said Deva. "Life's too short. Didn't you like any of my happy songs?"

"I enjoyed watching you sing."

He was looking at her again. Deva thought, He's trying to get up courage for a question. He's going to ask to see me later. Customers did ask. Occasionally, she did say yes. Now she spoke before he could. "I have to go. My daughter's asleep upstairs. She has school tomorrow."

"Your husband's a lucky man," he said.

"She's all mine."

"Then…can I offer you both a lift home?"

"Thanks. There's a taxi I use."

"My car's just around the corner."

Deva thought, He goes to AA. He's rather shy and rather sad. We have both been through something, alcohol or drugs, and whatever pain led to that. She trusted people from AA more than anyone.

"What sort of car?"

"A Porsche, I'm afraid."

Deva sighed. One of those Londoners then, with nasty money. The men who asked to take her home were often of this type. They were the ones she refused. "Of course, a Porsche," she lilted. "Does it even have room for my daughter?"

"There is a back seat. Made for a seven-year-old." Then he added, "It's not mine. My brother's. I usually take the Tube, but you go on late here."

This was in his favor.

He said, "No tricks."

"Then why bother?" she replied.

He shrugged. "Postponing being alone."

He's difficult to read, Deva thought. Not the normal play-boy. She had a moment of maternal compassion which drove away her fears, so that she said, "Well, at least you haven't been drinking. It's not close. Bloomsbury, the Kings Cross end."

"That's okay."

"Then be outside in ten minutes? I'll be carrying my daughter."

When they reached her front door, at the northern end of Bloomsbury, where the flat prices began to shade down, Deva struggled both to hold Nadia and to excavate her shoulder bag for her keys. "Take her," she said, delivering Nadia into Harry's arms, a solid little sleeping body softened by a blanket. Her head lodged itself against his shoulder, trusting him. One strand of dark hair had fallen across Nadia's eye and mouth, and Deva noticed Harry gently detach this from the film of moisture that held it, and join it to some other strands.

"I'll take her now," said Deva, the door unlocked. "*Obligada.*"

But he had been reluctant to give up tenderness, and said, "It's okay, I can carry her in for you." Nadia shifted in his arms, pushing her lips up against the fabric of his suit, a darkening spot of spittle growing there. He added, "We don't want to wake her."

Deva considered him for a long moment, then said, "Okay," pushing the door open with her foot. "Go ahead. It's upstairs." Why not? she thought. He's beautiful.

After Deva had tucked in Nadia, she went to the living room and found Harry looking out of the window at the damp street below, where a young couple was admiring the Porsche. They looked harmless.

"Well, you're still here," Deva observed. He did not reply, or move towards her, so she added, "You may as well relax, since you are. I suppose you want to stay, don't you?" She looked him in the eyes, until he nodded.

"Okay," she said. "I need a shower. There was no time at the club." When he did not move, she pointed with a dramatic clarity: "That's the bedroom. Just move anything I left on the bed. I wasn't expecting anyone."

"I wasn't expecting…" he began, but Deva had no patience for ambivalence so late at night and did not let him finish. She went to him and kissed him on the mouth, bumping her body up against his in the same movement, then dipping to slip through his arms before they could close on her. "Are you going to make me do everything?" she asked. "You invited yourself in. Give me ten minutes to clean up. You can wait for me in bed. And in the morning, if you don't mind, I would appreciate it very much if you could leave by six at the latest. Before Nadia wakes."

When Deva came into the bedroom wearing nothing but a towel wrapped around her hair, Harry was still in his shirt and trousers. He had done as instructed and moved the pile of Deva's clothes from bed to chair. She moved around him, domestic, easy in her nakedness. "Come on," she said, plucking at his shirt, "take those off. Are you shy?"

Under the duvet next to her, he kissed her with soft enquiry and she felt him hard against her thigh. She took him in hand. It was as important now that this was done promptly as that it was done well. She cut short the kiss, whispering sweetly into his ear, "It's late," subsiding down the bed to take him in her mouth. After only a few seconds—and Deva knew she was doing it well—he eased her away from him and pulled her back face to face.

"That's not necessary," he said.

"Maybe not," she replied. "Don't move," and she rolled over to straddle him, slipping him decisively inside herself.

Deva closed her eyes. He felt good in her as she churned against him, working for her orgasm, confident of delivering his. She'd sleep then. But Harry stopped her and broke her concentration by declaring, "No!" She opened her eyes and was perplexed to see he looked upset. She said that he could just come if he needed to, he shouldn't worry about her, she could take care of herself, at which he lifted her entirely off him and turned her on her back, holding her down and re-entering her, causing Deva to gasp, and then laugh, saying, "Hurry, Harry." But he didn't laugh with her. Instead, he held her down and held himself back, refusing Deva's terms, and insisting on his, which, it became apparent, involved time and deliberation. This irritated Deva, and they tussled. Even pressed down by the neck and resisting, Deva continued her little movements below, her accomplished flutterings, to finish things, so that their lovemaking became a battle between Harry's demand that this should be unhurried, and Deva's insistence that this should be sex, efficiently achieved, and that no man visiting her bed should gainsay her once she had so determined. They grappled, he emotional and delaying, she persistent and intent, until their minds fell out of the equation and their bodies joined in the making of oblivion. When Deva came, she felt Harry give himself up. But then, soon after, he pulled away and uttered a sound that was something like despair.

Then they lay still. Deva did not want to know about Harry's despair so late at night. With mock annoyance she pushed him away with the heels of both hands, saying, "Bastardo!"

Deva slept deeply and woke to the memory of sex, turning to look for the man responsible with some vague notion of continuation. But the bed was empty.

There was no note, no phone number, no message on her phone. He must have left before daybreak. Well, that made life simpler. But, still. All she found was a photo, not of him, but of a peaceful country scene, an old man picking daffodils, his back to the camera. Inexplicable. It might have fallen from a pocket when Harry piled his clothes on top of hers. She turned it over: Nothing on the back. No date. Who carried photos these days? In the end, she offered both Harry and the old man, a shrug. She put the photo on a shelf, and set about her day.

She thought he would probably call her, or turn up at the Miranda again. Deva sometimes asserted that once known she was not easy to forget, and she thought Harry might have found the night memorable enough. She did not know what she would do if he did contact her, whether or not her interest in him would persist. But she would have liked to be the one to choose. Harry, the silver Porsche, the moment of pathos, the moment of passion, all vanished as if they had never been. The version she now told Harry always ended at the Miranda.

Harry leaned back on the couch and said to Deva. "I think that the important thing about daffodils is that they make people happy. That's my opinion." In a gesture of finality, he pushed aside the photo of John without taking his attention from Deva's face.

"And?"

"You said you were a daffodil."

"Ah! I see." Deva wondered if this could be described as flirting. If it was, it felt uncomplicated. This was not the troubled man she first met at the Miranda.

"It's sunny," said Harry. "We should go outside."

"You want to go out? It's not daffodil season."

"No. No, not down there. Out on the terrace. The world is bigger out there."

"Okay, let's. You know, Harry, sometimes I wonder if you even want to discover your past." She had never said this before and it seemed like dangerous territory. She waited.

Harry considered this. "Well, I'm supposed to have one, aren't I? A past. Everyone else does. And it's the reason you're here, isn't it? So, I want to remember. But, you know, my head feels too full, even without a past. There's already a lot to know. A man doesn't want to eat if he feels full. Especially if he is blindfolded and doesn't know what's on the plate. I don't know what might be hidden in my memory. And today, I'm happy. So, no urgency."

They moved outside, sliding open the glass doors and closing them, then crossing the terrace to rest their elbows on the parapet. Shoulders close. Companionable. Ahead of them was the roofscape of London's accumulated shapes, colors, and textures. Light reflected off the glassy skyscrapers far to their left. Directly in front, the city cluttered into craze, then haze.

The Thames was somewhere there, but not easy to make out. Neither one of them attempted to name a landmark. Deva said, "It's true. You're more content when you're not trying to remember."

"Yes. Like now."

"But you did tell me repeatedly that you wanted to discover your purpose. You said you were convinced that you had a purpose and you wanted to discover it. It was important to you."

"I've said that repeatedly?"

"Most days, when you were still forgetting your days."

"I felt it again today, when I woke up. That there's something important I should be doing, but that I don't know what it is. Something important. As you say, a purpose. Do I need a past to have a purpose, do you think?"

"Perhaps. Maybe it's waiting for you there."

"What about you, Deva?"

"A purpose? No, I don't think that way. I'm a mother. I have work. I have friends. I like to sing. It fills my heart when I sing and people are happy. That's all. Actually, it fills my heart when it makes people sad too." She laughed. "Purpose sounds heroic. Heroic is usually stupid."

"Did you always sing? I'm sorry, Deva, I probably asked you before."

"Oh, you did. Several times. You know, I used to give you different answers to your questions each time you asked."

"You did that? You lied to me?" He sounded puzzled.

"I wasn't trying to mislead you. I kept finding new aspects of the truth. When I understood that you would forget by the next day it gave me the freedom to be inconsistent. Which seemed like more truth, not less. For example, you asked me about Nadia's father many times, and each time I gave you a slightly different answer."

"Different fathers?"

"No, different stories about the same father."

"I was going to ask you again."

"I know. And I'll answer again."

"Tell me about Nadia's father."

"Okay."

For a minute they looked out silently on the London night. "You know, Harry," said Deva, "it's supposed to be my job to listen to you, not the other way around."

He laughed. "I think I like your memories better than mine."

"How would you know?"

Harry inclined his head, conceding the point. Again, they fell into silence. Deva understood that Harry was happy to wait for her to be able to talk, and that in this there was a new balance of care between them.

"Harry?" she began.

"Yes?"

"When we were talking about daffodils, I said their name narcissus might mean narcotic. And I mentioned opium. Remember?"

"I do."

"And do you know what heroin is?"

"Yes. It comes from opium. Are we talking about Nadia's father now?"

"Yes. And me."

Deva took a breath, pushed her hands against the parapet, fixed her eyes on the darkening city view, not on Harry, and began. "I'd come to America from Brazil. About ten years ago, now. To Washington DC. I had a place as a graduate student at George Washington University, a good university. I was studying hard. Also, singing. Also, drinking and dancing, and hardly ever sleeping alone, hardly ever sleeping with the same man twice, to be honest, hardly ever sleeping for more than four or five hours a night. I was in my early twenties, driven by something, and too young to know what. I was exploiting my good health, which I can only have inherited from my father, since my mother was never strong. Also, I was looking for my father, another reason for being in Washington. I never did find him, by the way. No one in the government or the aid agencies knew of a Jim who had worked in the Amazon over twenty years before."

It was Andy, Deva explained, a gentle American boy, and not one of the many men she met dancing and drinking, who carefully, and with a steady hand, eased the heroin needle into the vein of her arm that first time, almost painlessly. He had first studied her arm with a quiet concentration while she regarded his face, the sensitive features, the soft beard running wild. Quietly spoken Andy with his unutilized law degree and a father in the US senate. Andy, who, because he knew his father, had no taste for power himself, the kindest man she had met out of the hundreds she had met during her first few years in America.

Deva found Andy, not at a nightclub or a party girl party, but walking his small black and white dog near Dupont Circle at two in the morning as she was returning home, alone for once, and not looking forward to her dark night. "I like your dog," she said, and bent to pet the friendly mutt, who was considering a lamppost. Andy had smiled and said only, "That's Gilbert, Gilbert the dog," offering calm against her restless energy. He was high he told her later, but it seemed to Deva at that moment that he was just serene, a man not wanting anything from her but still able to save her from the lonely night. She lingered, still dressed for nightclub dancing, the perspiration from it cooling her now, her dress backless under the light coat, and she fell in with the stuttering amble dictated by Gilbert until Andy stopped in front of a handsome apartment building. "I live here," he said, in explanation, then, as if he were genuinely curious about, but disinterested in, her answer, he asked, "Do you want to come up?" The building looked comfortably afflu-ent, more enticing than her own meager place, and she would not be alone. "Yes," Deva said. "Okay."

She slept with Andy that night without anything happening between them, not even conversation, the longest, deepest sleep she had known in years. In the morning she thought to ask his name.

There was nothing of the caricature addict about Andy. He worked in a bookstore, arrived on time, was attentive to customers and efficient: a gracious, quietly spoken young man who held himself back from success because he had seen what success was like. What he wanted, when work was done, was to eat simply and slightly, take his dog Gilbert for a walk around the block, and then shoot up into an easy bliss. Once in the morning, once at night—like coffee and cocktails, they said—not too much, not out of control. Andy became Deva's first real friend in America. The men she had met all wanted sex or possession, and the women, often party girls like herself, but not as bright, were shallow and sometimes jealous of the way Deva's intimate manner promised everything to men, and quickly, and the way that men were so easily captured by this promise, and the truth in it. Unlike many of the women, Deva could shed her men and hangovers each morning, and work hard at her studies by day—satisfying the sharp appetite of her mind—even as she played fast and loose with actual class attendance. Her grades were excellent.

Andy was almost feminine in manner, and though actually unambiguously heterosexual, he exercised this tendency rarely. His body was lean and wiry, which Deva preferred to the gym-manufactured bodies of many young Americans, and though he was well endowed, he was not much interested in the arousal that best demonstrated this, evidencing an agnosticism towards sex that was, to Deva, a novelty. It was like having a girlfriend but without the competition, all this by the grace of Andy's greater interest in the profounder pleasures of heroin. They hung out together, listened to music, touched easily, doing not much, and before long, with her customary fearlessness, Deva had persuaded Andy to slide a needle carefully into her vein, so that she discovered a relief that she had not imagined could be possible in her life. Andy had asked her several times if she was sure that this was what she really wanted, and each time she had replied, yes, she wanted to experience what he experienced. Now, she could see the danger, because this was as things should be, a great breathing out at last, after she had held her breath for half a lifetime. Only now did she acknowledge the tension that was in her, the running from something, the willful forgetting of something, the busy mind that kept the something out, because now none of that mattered. Heroin transcended all of it, wiped away at a stroke, guilt, regret, and pain. She looked at Andy studying her as the heroin went to work in her that first time, watching the rearrangement of her features, and, after he had taken care of himself, he lay himself down on the floor next to her, clothed and separate and joined. "Better than sex," murmured Deva, resting her fingers on Andy's cheek in gratitude.

Like Andy, and against popular prejudice, Deva did not overnight turn into a depraved street junkie. She continued to function in the world and in fact felt better. She completed her master's degree, and, taking singing lessons instead, she sensed that her performances were gaining a new maturity and professionalism. Deva no longer woke up disoriented in the strange beds of foreign men whose names she would never remember. She drank less and did not enter her days by pushing aside the heavy curtains of hangovers. The days entered her by a needle in a vein. She went through them effectively with the craving building. But this was not a terrible craving since it was a craving that would be reliably satisfied each night with Andy, and his reliable supply of high-quality heroin, guaranteed by the trust fund the senator had settled on him, to be done with him. Deva loved this so much, this dependable island of peace discovered within her driven life.

Though Andy was addicted, and she knew that she had also become addicted, it was not too high a cost, or too pressing a problem. The heroin was good. Their money was sufficient. If their usage increased over time, it was a barely perceptible increase. They dream-walked through the world, and together at home—Deva moved in with Andy before the end of their first month—the domesticity was private and sweet. Though sex was rare, they knew each other's bodies well, stroking, tapping, uncovering shy but hospitable veins in overlooked crannies. Andy explored her for this examination with fingertips more sensitive and skillful than those of any other intimate, the gentlest and most solicitous of lovers, the one most able to give the fullest satisfaction. Her love for Andy reached out to the damage of his childhood, the crudely bullying father scornful of his son's sensitivity, the neglectful alcoholic mother who did nothing to protect him, her duties as wife requiring only that on specified occasions she appear in public sober, slim, and smiling. His damaged childhood had brought him to this comfort, as had hers. She loved him for his unfailing consideration, his unforced fidelity—what was there to be found for him in another woman?—and for the wealth, indirectly provided by the American electorate, which enabled the heroin without any of the terrible requirements to earn, beg, or steal.

They loved this way for two years, while Deva's studies were completed and her singing career rose to modest success, and then subsided from her carelessness towards this success. The opinions of her peers and mentors were generally approval of the new quiet and steadiness in Deva's life. While she studied, Andy continued to work in the bookstore for his low and entirely unnecessary wage. At home, they walked Gilbert, made simple meals, or ordered in, and listened to music on Andy's expensive sound system while lying on the bed, the couch, or the floor. Little pieces of gauze, each with a red spot on it, were to be found in odd places around the apartment, like fading Japanese flags, reminders of their loyal allegiance to another sovereignty, and markers of time served.

A year or so after Deva completed her master's degree in anthropology and international development, while she was letting her singing career go, during the time when she was considering where her life might next take her, but finding it impossible to imagine leaving sweet Andy and his heroin, she returned home one evening to find him lying still and dead on their living room floor, an empty syringe and little Japanese flag next to him. He was supposed to wait for her return before shooting up; that was their habit. For all his carefulness, and for all the outward regularity of his life, here was Andy, the senator's son, lying dead and peaceful, either from an overdose, or from a bad batch of heroin. She shook him, swore in Portuguese, pleaded in Portuguese, and started mouth-to-mouth resuscitation before accepting that Andy was dead, and cold. A rush of hysterical tears overcame her, which she snapped shut. Instead, she kneeled by Andy's body and prayed—the first time in many years—for Andy's eternal soul. Let him have peace. Let him have heaven. She explained to God, in case he did not already know, that Andy was a kind and gentle man, with a kind and injured heart. God should not be taken in by the bad reputation of addicts down here on earth, but should reward him with heaven above.

Gilbert the dog, who was at first agitated, then cowering, now brought Deva back to the present by making a sudden rush at her and biting her on the ankle fiercely enough to draw blood. Deva swatted him away, astonished by, and understanding, this completely uncharacteristic behavior. Poor Gilbert; his world was on its head. She understood what she must do, also against precedence: she must dial 911 and deal with the authorities.

She could have called Andy's family, but preferred the authorities. Deva had met Andy's parents only twice and each time was tolerated only as the expression of the unsuitable wasteful life led by their son, which they expected one day to change, never acknowledging his addiction. She would let the authorities deal with the family. She went to the phone, then stopped. Half of the heroin Andy had used was set aside for her. Today he had not waited. There could be no moment when she would need it more. If the heroin was good, it would help her get through this; if it was bad, then she was in it with Andy to the last. She went through the familiar rituals of preparation, then found and mastered a tricky vein in her ankle and squeezed the syringe steadily. The familiar tide rose in her. She waited, lying down next to Andy's dead body, until she was convinced that she was not going to die. Then she dialed 911.

That was the last heroin for Deva. The police were kind to her—she was after all very pretty—and she had completed the formalities before it wore off. She dosed up on codeine, but the pain had already started, the aches, the dripping nose of withdrawal flu, and, worst, the twitching deep in her muscles that kept her moving and stopped her sleeping. All of her screamed with hurt. For ten days she took her punishment in the apartment where Andy died—bleak and awful and a sort of death—and by the time the man hired by Andy's father came around to take Andy's things, including Gilbert, and tell her to get out, she was able to get out. She packed her things and bought an air ticket to Brazil. University College London had accepted her for its PhD program, but she asked for a post-ponement because, against all likelihood, she was pregnant with Andy's child. Their sex had been so rare that precautions had seemed ridiculous.

Back in Brazil, the idea of heroin introduced itself to her a thousand times a day, but each day the little Nadia growing inside her had made her face it down, and had saved her.

Deva had stopped talking. The air on the terrace had grown cool. "So," she said at last, "that was Nadia's father. The long version. He was dead before she was born." After more silence, she added, "God, Harry, you should have stopped me. It's dark. Are you all right?"

Harry had not moved and did not move now. His eyes remained on the horizon. Their shoulders touched where they leaned on the parapet together. Deva turned towards him and saw that while she had been lost in her story, Harry's cheeks had become damp. But when as last he replied to Deva's question, he said, "I'm all right. I feel good." Then after a moment, "I shouldn't, should I?"

"I don't know, Harry. What feels good?"

"It's not your story. That made me sad. I felt like you were in me. Maybe I feel good because for the first time I know what it's like to have a past, even though it isn't mine. I can almost understand what it's like to have memories, to have feelings about them. The past is feelings, isn't it? Not just memories?"

Deva subtly increased the pressure of her shoulder against his, and still regarding him, said quietly, "Yes, of course. That's why people sometimes want to forget. But maybe you feel good because you were doing good. You were doing me good. Listening. I've never talked like that before."

"I did nothing."

"Not many people can do that sort of nothing. You listen with your whole person. You've no idea how rare it is."

Deva watched his face—always transparent these days—as he puzzled this. He considered something, then shook his head, then considered something else. Finally, Harry asked quietly, "Do you think this nothing might be my purpose? Listening? Doing nothing?"

"Perhaps." Deva laughed lightly—a musical sound—and kissed him on the cheek. "Perhaps it is." They embraced, everything gentle, everything careful, nothing claimed, then separated with an equal care. It wasn't sex. "It hadn't occurred to me before," said Deva, "but actually you remind me a bit of Andy. You have the same light touch. He could remember his past, of course, his childhood, but he never wanted to talk about it. He wanted to forget. There were things he could not bear to remember. I loved Andy."

Harry nodded.

Deva said, "I've made you sad. What was it? Do you know?"

"It was sad thinking of you. Losing you to heroin. You losing Andy."

"Maybe something in your own past too?"

Harry let his head fall into his hands, his elbows braced by the parapet. "Of course, I don't know," he said quietly.

"I'm sorry, Harry," said Deva. "That was stupid of me."

Deva's first phone call to John was awkward. She struggled to explain that a man who John seemed unable to place, living on a different continent, believed that John's presence was crucial to the recovery of his damaged memory. As she described Harry's accident and inability to travel, indeed his inability to cope with the street outside his own home, she heard her own words as far-fetched. John's response was, at first, silence. Then she mentioned the photo that had made the connection. "I don't know of any photo like that," John said flatly.

This John, Deva decided, was a hard nut to crack: uncommunicative, incurious, skeptical, and unimpressed by mentions of Harry's luxurious home, or of hospitality in London. She reported this back to Dr Elliot, who was quick to suggest that she might have more luck in person.

She told Harry of her conversations with John. He thought for a moment, then smiled and said, "Curmudgeon." Deva laughed, liking that this man, John Bradley, could be so summarized by Harry in a single comic word. It made her task seem to be a competition between the deployment of her charm and John's innate resistance to charm. Deva was cautiously optimistic.

She asked Harry his opinion. "So, should I go?"

He closed his eyes before replying, more tentative than she had expected. Finally, he said, "If you don't mind. If you can bring him here." He closed his eyes again.

"But?" prompted Deva

"I don't know," said Harry. "There's something complicated in it. I don't know what. Perhaps you should be careful."

"I will be. I'm a good judge of people, don't you think? And I've had some practice with strangers and careful."

Harry nodded his assent, looking thoughtful. "You'll tell me about all that one day," he said.

Deva arrived at Omar's Bookstore Café before the appointed time, so that when John walked in and cast his glance around, she had long been absorbed into the café's morning table of lively international women, well blended with them, talking English, talking bad Spanish, and with the other Brazilian there, who had spotted her immediately and pulled her in, talking Portuguese. Deva's laugh, which started high and ended husky, added a new note to the cafe, as did the look of her, dressed for New Hampshire in a flimsy green and orange dress. When she sat, she wrapped a luxurious scarf around herself, covering bare shoulders. Heels of course. Jewelry of course. Smiling of course. Two men lingered at the table over general greetings, then stayed to pull up chairs, held easily by the table's new energy and the brush of Deva's eyes, even while she was becoming cozy with the touch of her new sisters. A star in plain sight.

Deva was nervous. It was unlike her, and annoyed her. This was her first visit back to the US since returning to Brazil to have Nadia, seven years earlier. Andy's death was still fresh then. Still, this was different from those last grim days in Washington, a friendly New England college town, and here she was talking, laughing, answering all the questions—yes, she had a doctorate in anthropology from the University of London, and, no, it had been years since she had been back to Brazil, and, yes, really, what she said was true, she also sang in a nightclub, they didn't really want to hear something, did they, so early in the day, well okay then. She offered a few phrases of a song in a low voice, which nevertheless stopped the conversation, as if they had not really believed until then that her singing might be wonderful. And all the time that she was talking, laughing, singing, charming, her deeper thoughts were on the man she was about to meet. She knew his back so well, cardiganed and bent over daffodils in a rustic garden, and through Harry, she thought she also knew something of the cumudgeon's inner life, the hurt and loneliness. There was no reason to be nervous.

She picked him out before he picked her out, an achievement that he later said impressed him. His eyes had passed over the usual table of women, scanning the room for a woman alone and he was thus convinced that Deva had not yet arrived. He ordered his coffee and found his table under the high book-shelves towards the back. Deva, by then, was so completely embraced by the other women that she was concealed in plain sight: an old friend visiting, the focus of the day's interest.

While Deva talked, her eyes checked around for older men. The one she settled on was dressed in good clothes, a herringbone jacket well broken in. His posture was good too. The photo had not suggested good posture. The short gray hair, seen from the front, was brusquely cut, giving a purpose-ful impression without any of the vulnerability suggested from behind. The girl at the counter smiled at him, but he barely smiled back. He was a handsome older man with a worn face. Deva thought that the lines fanning out from his eyes were more likely caused by squinting into the sun than by laughing. If Harry was right about this man being in a crisis, it did not show. Nor did he seem to be on the lookout for anyone—for her—but instead, when he turned and sat, took in the cafe with only mild interest before opening his glasses and giving full attention to his newspaper. But by then Deva knew he was the one. His back had informed on him when he walked away from the counter, the unconscious man revealed by it, making a fool of the conscious one assembled at his front. Deva was certain.

To her new Brazilian friend, Deva whispered, "Don't look now, but that man at the far end of the room, with the short gray hair, reading the paper, do you know him?"

"He's always here," she replied. "We don't really know him. Sometimes we make things up about him. We had an argument once about whether a man his age could be attractive. But recently he seemed to be letting himself go. He looks good today. Why do you ask?"

"I think," said Deva, picking up her bag, "that I need to meet him."

The table, along with much of the café, watched in amazement, as Deva walked directly down the long room, her heels emphatic, to the man no one ever talked to, and held out her hand for him to shake.

By the time she reached him, John was not caught by surprise. Over his glasses, he saw her detach herself from the group and immediately he understood his mistake, thinking, "I'm out of practice," before also registering in a quick succession: Yes, she's striking. The face is lovely, and the smile disarming; I have been too much alone and should be careful. By the time John stood to take Deva's hand, he had taken her measure, and his own.

"I'm Deva," said Deva. "I think you must be John Bradley."

"Well, it's good to meet you, Deva. You've come a long way. I do hope you will not be disappointed. Can I get you a coffee?"

"Thank you. Espresso."

"Single, double?"

"Double."

"Good. Then excuse me for a minute. They can be a little slow. It's not Italy." He made his way to the counter. People were looking at him in new ways since the arrival of Deva. It didn't feel bad.

"You said," John began when he was settled back, "that this is about helping a friend of yours. This man I've never heard of. With the mysterious complaint. I'd like to help, of course, but it's hard to understand how. You say he's lost his memory?"

"I know it's strange. It must seem bizarre. But he's convinced he must have known you."

"And he gave you my name?"

"Yes, like I said on the phone, it's the one thing he remembers. And it's even more strange, really. He knew your name just from looking at a photo of your back."

"Okay, Deva. Peculiar. Let's say, I'm hooked. But he can't say where he knows me from? Harry, right? No last name."

"No, he doesn't know where. He's forgotten everything. Harry is all I have for a name."

"And he's English?"

"Well, he's from London, and he seems like a native English speaker. But he doesn't look like traditional English. More a mixture, like me. So, something else in his past."

"But you're not related in any way?"

"Oh no. He's definitely not Brazilian. I met him once before he lost his memory. He came to the club where I work. Of course, he doesn't remember that either. His English is very good. He's a well-educated man."

"You have his picture?"

"On my phone. Here."

John took the phone and studied it. He said, "Good-looking young man. No. Nothing. Sorry."

"He's very nice," said Deva.

"And he's sure he knows me?"

"Yes. He's convinced he must have known you. Because you're in the photo I mentioned. It was his photo. But it's not just that. The photo stirs something up in him. He's been obsessed."

"Can I see the photo?"

"Sure. It's the next one. It is you, isn't it?"

"Where did you say this came from again?"

"When I first met him, he left an old-fashioned print behind. He dropped it and I found it later."

"Well, it's me all right."

"And your garden. You have daffodils?"

"Yes, but no one takes photos of me."

"Not even your family."

"No." John shook his head. "I live alone. I'm retired. Quiet life."

There was the sadness. Harry was right.

"Harry can't explain it, but he believes that you are very

important to him in some way. And he feels that you may be his best hope for recovering his memory. His doctor agrees, by the way. You and I seem to be the only people connected to his past. It's a complete mystery. But it's also fascinating, don't you think? Will you come?"

"What exactly is it you want me to do?"

"Just come to London and meet him. Spend some time with him. To see if he's right about you being important. You might jog his memory, or he might realize he's made a mistake. It's a long shot, but nothing else is working. He can pay you. He's rich. Do you have the time?"

"Well, I'd be lying if I said I didn't have the time. There's the house, of course—the garden."

Deva chose not to reply, so that at last, he asked, "What exactly is your role, Deva?"

"Keeping him company. Answering his questions. Research. Easing him back into life. I'm an anthropologist. I'm being paid too. It's a job."

"So, not a personal thing?"

"Not really."

"Just a job?"

"Not just anything. I care about him. There's something very special about Harry that makes you want to help him. Or maybe just be around him. He has a presence. I think you'll understand when you met him. If you do come, you can stay with us. He has this stunning modernist home on a roof off Baker Street in London. There's lots of room. I live there too now."

"A presence?"

Deva shrugged. "Yes. I think that's the right word. An aura. A simplicity. He never lies. I think it doesn't even occur to him."

"Okay, look, how does he even know his name is Harry if he can't remember anything?"

"Well, the doctors know. And I know. He might not know it for himself. But his memory is starting to improve."

"In what way?"

"When I first arrived, he used to forget everything about

every day when he went to sleep at night. Each morning he
started a new life. He woke every day with this fresh sense of
mission. But now he remembers yesterdays. That started at
about the time he came up with your name. Now he's got three
weeks of yesterdays. Three weeks of memories. Still nothing
from before."

"I've read about cases like that."

"So, you're interested?"

"Let me think about it. Tell me about yourself. Where are
you from originally?"

They talked of this and that. John had worked in international aid, he said, and knew something about Brazil. He even
knew something about fado and its history in Portugal. He was
well informed, had opinions about anthropology, and apparently found the subject of Deva's doctoral thesis fascinating. They
slipped into a hedged enjoyment: an intelligent woman had
found an intelligent man over coffee. Deva's morning slipped
into something close to pleasure.

No, he was divorced, John said, when Deva's interest pitched
that way. Two children. In their forties now. "They grow away
from you," he said. "Estranged, these days." There was the
bleakness again. Then he perked up to ask, "And is your daughter as charming as her mother?"

"More charming," Deva assured him, thinking, So, this John
is also a man, and adding, "But then she's seven."

"Okay, let me sleep on it," John said, as they parted. "Can
you give me a day or two? I know you have to get back to
London and your daughter. If you like, we can meet here
Wednesday morning. Same time. But I have to say, Deva, you've
made today a lot more interesting than most of my days. More
pleasant too."

"Good. Please try to come, John. Visit London. Meet Harry.
Meet my daughter. Come and hear me sing. Why wouldn't you?
We can fly business class on Harry's money. I expect he'd agree
to first, if you insisted. And you might even give a man his life
back. Who knows? Save his life, really. Imagine! You've nothing

better to do, have you? You could do some good. A lot of good. And you're curious now, aren't you? Isn't your life a bit quiet, John? Be honest. If it all turns out to be for nothing, what have you lost?"

While she spoke, Deva rested her arms on the table and leaned forward to take both of John's hands in hers, the table edge pressing into her. John's hands were rough, the joints swollen, and Deva thought of him working alone in his garden, and how Harry had insisted that all of the man's body was hurting. She thought that there was not enough love to go around in this world and that some people got left out. "Do come," she said. "I wish you would."

John counseled himself not to speak. He was unused to touch. He grimaced, then managed evenly, "I need to sleep on it, Deva."

"Yes. Good." She released his hands and leaned back.

"There's the matter of messenger and message, and all that," he said, his smile turning wry.

"No difference. The messenger is here because Harry is worth it. That's the message."

John called Gwen that afternoon and described the approach from the Brazilian.

"Good," said Gwen. "Let her charm you."

"I want to agree on Wednesday. Can you get confirmation by then?"

"I'll call you back, John."

An hour later Gwen was on the phone. "They're pleased. You'll report to the British there, though not really of course. Hardly any instructions. You'll find your own way."

"They're trusting me, then?"

"You'd almost think so, wouldn't you?"

Deva and John took a daytime flight from Boston and, by the time they reached Baker Street that night, Harry was already asleep, leaving Deva and Mrs. Slater to settle John into a secluded guest room. The next morning Harry insisted that he be the one to tap on John's door and call out the invitation to breakfast, recalling the way his own new life started in the confusion at Mrs. Slater's strident voice, and wanting to make sure that his own invitation was more welcoming.

When John joined them in the living room, rested and wearing a jacket in case so impressive a home implied formality, Harry rose from the breakfast table to greet him, full of warmth. "John, I'm so grateful you agreed to come. Thank you. I thought you might not. Let me see you. You know, so far I only know you from your back."

Harry took John's hand, looked briefly at his face, found nothing remarkable there, and laughed, then turned towards the table, pleased to have this to offer his visitor, a spread of food, a view of London, the delightful little Nadia, the already met Deva. Less than two months ago Harry had been a stranger in this world, with no past. Now he had this life, this nub of history, and something to offer a solitary guest. He kept hold of John's hand, not releasing it until he had placed him at the table, then fussed to settle him and received assurance that all that John might want was before him, thus freeing his guest from any requirement for formal speech. Deva observed that Harry had the instincts of a host, evidence, she thought, of some earlier social standing, probably in a culture more hospitable than the English.

Looking around the table, Harry thought, This is my family,

trying out the notion. It already felt more fully formed by the addition of a fourth seat at the table, three generations spanned. He watched John reach for toast, then caught Deva's eye and smiled. They shared the conviction of this man's loneliness. Harry and Deva would bring him back to life. It would be a happy task.

John looked around the table and had the ridiculous idea that in this new, light place, high above London, he might be exempted from all that had gone before. He was surprised by Harry, who looked fit and at ease, a more successful man than himself in these regards. There was no sign of serious injury, nor any obvious need for help. Harry's attention, Deva's warmth—this disconcerting show of unguarded affection towards him—rendered him quiet with a non-specific shame.

In the lull among the grown-ups, Nadia took the opportunity to fix the new arrival's eye and say, "John, watch me," upon which she slid from her chair and cartwheeled across the room, then cartwheeled back, to grin at her surprised new friend.

"That's very impressive," John mustered.

"I can do somersaults too."

She was poised to redouble her display when Deva brought it to a halt, saying, "Nadia, that's enough of showing off your underwear. You need to finish your breakfast and get dressed for school." Then she reinforced these instructions in Portuguese, at greater length and with more color. Deva turned back to John to laugh, "What can I say? She's my daughter."

The logic of the situation would make Deva and Harry lovers, but seeing them together John was not sure. Deva sat close to Harry, and she clearly liked him, but the bait of her was never taken so that its offering had the freedom of no consequence. There was no tension between them and John played with the idea that Harry was homosexual and uninterested, but understood that his mind was just trawling for simplicities, and he could not make that thinking work. Deva looked relaxed. Harry looked content.

On the plane, John had regarded Deva sitting next to him, her eyes closed, the skin of her shoulder golden, a red bra strap showing, and thought she would be an effective honey trap, except that these days no one would think him worth trapping, nor bet on his appetite for honey. She seemed to be genuinely fond of this Harry. Harry—could he really be his old friend's boy?

In turn, Deva had looked at John when his eyes were closed, sitting straight in the seat, head centered on the rest. It was a strong, disciplined face, but spent. She could find little present life in it. He suddenly started and then turned to catch her look, rather sternly she thought. She smiled to disarm him. John rubbed his eyes, looked down and finding much of Deva's bare thighs curled up there, looked back up. She saw that he had tried for sleep, but failed. She thought that there was a hint of pleading in his look.

At the breakfast table, Harry talked mostly to Nadia, responding to her chatter and softly coaxing her, as she came and went. She was running late for school, delayed by the novelty of John and then an indecision over her outfit for the day. It ended up as pink tights, purple jacket, frilly green skirt, blue earrings, blue nails. She had been determined to ignore her mother's fashion advice and ended up triumphant at both her independence and the ensemble's unlikely success. "My daughter," said Deva, resigned and proud, as Nadia reappeared in the outfit's final iteration. Deva touched up her own make-up with a hand-held mirror, saying, "Okay, men. We have to go. I'll be back in about an hour. Nadia, bring that toast with you. Harry, are you sure you'll be all right?"

Harry looked over at John. "I'm sure. I have John for company."

John's thoughts about Nadia, after being obliged to watch her fashion show, were that she was too cute, too Latin. He did not approve of small girls wearing earrings, and Nadia at seven, had flashed her eyes in too precise an imitation of her mother. There was the nail varnish too, all the trappings of adult allure prematurely passed down. Then he asked himself why he was disapproving like a father, or grandfather? He had no business here with Nadia, and no qualifications for fatherhood.

When the clattering departures of Deva and Nadia had faded into quiet, Harry turned to John and smiled. "Please, you must make yourself at home. We can talk later. There's no hurry. You can explore the house if you like. That's what I did on my first day. Nothing is forbidden, except going through that door. Mrs. Slater and the kitchen are beyond that door. Foreign lands."

"You explored? Isn't this your house?"

"So I understand. I meant that on the first day that I remember, I remember exploring. And according to Mrs. Slater I did the same all the days before that. You know I was in a coma for a while after the car accident. This is a new life for me."

"You don't remember anything at all?"

"From before. No, not really. But that could change. It used to be that I forgot each day, every day. And because I had no sense that there had been a previous day, apparently I never felt the loss. It was more tiresome for the others, no doubt. Deva especially. I'm curious, of course, about the past." He smiled at John and guided him out onto the patio, into the morning sun. They went to the wall and dipped to peer down at the street.

John said, "I'd like to help. But I don't know how I can."

"You can't help but help. In one way or another. I'm sure of it." Harry paused, then said, "If you like, you could take a walk outside. Regent's Park is quite close. But if you do, I will unfortunately not be able to join you. I can't go outside—it seems there's too much going on down there for my brain to manage. Dr Elliot—he's my doctor—has a name for it, but I can't remember what it is. If you'd like company, you could wait for Deva to return."

He is charming, John thought. Charming and considerate.

"You look very well for someone who was so seriously injured."

Harry smiled warmly, as if this was a shared delight. "I am well, I think. Except," he tapped his head, "no memory. And I sleep a lot. And I can't go outside, or do anything exciting." But this too appeared to please him.

John thought that Harry seemed like a happy man. His eyes were clear and his movements relaxed and supple. He was the sort of attractive, good-natured, quietly assured man that people liked. By comparison John felt old, stiff, and burdened. Not charming. He wondered if some of Harry's glow might come from medications.

Harry said, more serious now, "John, I hope you will stay with us for a while. You'll feel better, I think. And we'd all like it."

Harry took out the photo and put it down in the center of the coffee table. Deva said, "This is the famous photo, John. The one that led us to you."

John studied it. "Yes, I saw it on your phone. Still, it's different seeing the actual print. A novelty, these days. That's my backyard all right. And that's me bending over. Quite recent, I think. Do you think you took it, Harry?"

Harry shrugged. "I only know that Deva says I had it and lost it. And that somehow it's important."

"It's strange. Why would anyone take a photo of me in my garden? It looks like it could be taken from the woods. It's…a bit disconcerting."

"You can't think why someone might have taken it?" asked Deva

"No. I don't have visitors. Just the oil delivery man. My mailbox is on the other side of the road."

"Of course," said Harry, smiling, "I was hoping that I'd been a visitor and you'd recognize me immediately."

"I'm sorry. I wish that were true. I can't believe you managed to find me just from this."

"It was a lot of work," said Deva. "A lot of botany."

John thought about it. It made no sense.

"You're sure you don't know me at all?" asked Harry.

John turned to him. Harry's features were even, cosmopolitan, open. You expected dark eyes, but they were green. He tried to see his old friend's face in him, but couldn't. Even with imagining a big beard on it, this face seemed of a different, softer type. He said, "If I did know you, it would have been a long time ago. I used to travel a lot with my work, but that was decades ago. Perhaps you looked different then. You would have been young. Unless you came to America recently, of course. But then I'd probably remember. When I was working internationally, I met hundreds of people—thousands—in all sorts of countries, and I've forgotten nearly all of them. So, who knows…? I could have met you somewhere, I suppose. But I'm sure we never knew each other well."

"Do you remember picking the daffodils?" asked Deva.

John turned back to the photo and did not reply.

Harry said, "I could tell you loved the flowers."

John did not react, then at last said quietly, "This is uncomfortable. My back is facing whoever took the photo and I don't know they're there. It feels exposed."

Deva said that if there was anything he needed to know about daffodils, he only had to ask her, since Harry had turned her into an expert.

John ignored this, his eyes still on the picture. "I'm cutting them," he said. "I've only cut the daffodils once."

"So, you remember?"

John nodded. "I do."

Harry said, "You're lost in admiring that one particular daffodil you're holding, aren't you? You're not moving."

"No, I'm not." It was extraordinary. The photo had been taken at the exact time of his episode, his mini-stroke—whatever it was—when he had been most helpless.

Harry waited, then said, "I've no idea how I knew your name from the photo. It just popped out." He reached down and tilted the picture more towards himself, as if there might still be something more to learn. He said, "At first I thought you were not moving because you were thinking. Then I thought that you were not moving because you were not thinking." He looked from the photo to John for confirmation. John's face was blank. "It seemed like you were in a sort of trance, your mind was somehow torn open—that was my feeling. I've no idea why I would think that just by looking at your back." He laughed.

For a moment it seemed to John that it was not ridiculous that Harry should know him, that his guileless way might be exactly the way to know him, and also that it might not be so bad to be known in this way. "Actually," he said, "as a matter of fact, something did happen around that time." He hesitated while the others waited, then continued. "My brain sort of stopped working. I lost consciousness for a moment. I think it might be called a mini-stroke. A brain fart. Sorry, Deva." Deva gave a shrug to show she was unshockable. "I just went blank. I'm not sure for how long. Then I recovered. It wasn't that serious."

He was being honest now, or almost, against a lifelong habit. The thought struck him out of the blue, that he had never lied to his children. He had not told them everything, of course, but he had never lied. They had been too young to care about his work. To own any positive thought about his fathering was exceptional, and he registered this novelty before returning to the subject at hand. "It wasn't unpleasant, the blankness, as far as I can recall. When things started up again, that wasn't so good."

While John stared out the window, piecing together his thoughts, Harry and Deva stayed quiet, sharing the understanding that there might be more to come.

John decided on the safer course. "Strangely, I do remember what I was thinking just before my mind went blank. I was looking at the flower and thinking about how the world was becoming hotter—global warming, you know. The daffodils were very early. I was going over in my mind how we humans had brought ourselves to the brink of catastrophe. The way we had done it bit by bit, one thing following another, faster and faster without ever seeing clearly, or being able to stop ourselves. We just couldn't help it. Maybe my head just got too cold while I was thinking about global warming. Ironic, eh? I'd forgotten to put on a hat."

"And afterwards?" Harry asked quietly.

"Afterwards?"

"After the blank."

John shook his head and grimaced. "Oh, just a rush of crazy thoughts then. Horrors, really. My brain started back up again all at once. My whole life came at me. The worst parts, mainly, I have to say. It was like I'd been holding them back by thinking, and then I'd dropped my guard and they all rushed in."

Harry said, "I knew that."

John gave him a sharp look.

"From the photo, I mean. I could sense that."

"Don't worry, John," said Deva, reaching out to put her hand on his arm. "He does that. It's a bit unnerving. Whatever happened to Harry seems to have made him super intuitive. It's a bit strange, but in a good way." Now she touched Harry's arm with her other hand.

"Maybe there's not enough of my own life to fill my head," explained Harry. "So, there's room for other things. I think that must be it. But I'm not being a good host, taxing you with all this the day after you arrived. Let's stop now."

"In any case," said Deva, "I have to go. I have to meet Nadia. Why don't you come with me, John? Have a walk and some fresh air. We can take Nadia to see the ducks."

"The memories," said John abruptly, ignoring the interruptions, "were all like flowers. Blooming. Approaching and expanding, engulfing me. But all horrors. Mockeries of flowers. It's only just occurred to me, that it might have been because I was staring at an actual flower." He looked up at Harry, and said, "Sorry, but I can't describe exactly what I saw." He heard the break of emotion in his own voice and wondered at it, that this was so far from the covert assessment of Harry that he had imagined for himself, this entire surrender of the upper hand.

Harry replied as if he had been asked a question. "John, there is absolutely nothing you could tell us that would make us not want you here."

Deva looked at Harry, taken aback by this declaration. And there was the "us" too, Harry also speaking for her. Then she turned back to John and saw his upset, and wished to save him from it. She said, "Come on, John. This is a bit much for your first day. Come and see the ducks. It's not even raining for once."

Harry watched as Deva took John's arm and leaned into him, as if she needed his support for the journey down the steps, John in thrall to Deva, enlivened by her, his carriage straightening as they progressed. She's wonderful, he thought—and was reminded of another recent departure, his own, the waving hands from his life in dreams, and the mission of transcendent importance that he was being dispatched to discover. Perhaps John would reveal it. Perhaps it was the global warming he talked about. Then he laughed at himself: a man unable to leave his own home, imagining to save the world.

Harry was wrapped up in a duvet from chin to toe, lying outside on one of terrace loungers, when John found him. It was late morning and the weather was gray, moist, and uninviting.

John had woken at two with a violent dream in which he was intent on killing a furry lap dog by hitting it repeatedly with a rake, as if it were deadly and a threat to him. There had been something like it once in South America, not him with the rake, and a snake not a dog. It was hours before sleep agreed to take him in again and then he slept late—was allowed to sleep late. He found a tray with a flask of coffee, a covered glass of orange juice, and a plate with two croissants, tucked just inside his door, and he thought that it was probably Harry who had put it there. When he finally emerged into the light of the house, it was perfectly quiet and seemed entirely empty, like a ghost ship sailing through the sky with he its only passenger. Nadia would be at school, of course, and Deva might be at a rehearsal at the Miranda, or on any number of errands. Mrs. Slater would be doing whatever she did when she disappeared into her private quarters, preparing meals for them, perhaps just putting her feet up, or perhaps reporting to her masters in intelligence. She was efficient and considerate, but did not invite friendship. Following the tradition of English housekeepers, he supposed. Also, following good professional practice, of course. The house had seemed empty, but now here was Harry on the terrace, quiet in his cocoon.

Looking down at the unmoving body, John wondered if Harry's composure was sleep or unconsciousness. Where did Harry's mind go when it daydreamed with so few memories from which to make dreams?

"Join me," murmured Harry, without opening his eyes. "Pull up a lounger. There's a pile of duvets behind you. I think lying here warm in the cool air is even better than lying here warm in the warm air. Like sweet and sour together can be better than sweet or sour alone."

The two men lay silently next to each other while below them, heard but out of sight, London hustled through its working day. John felt he should be doing something with more purpose and at first fidgeted—it was less than an hour since he got out of bed—but nothing of the kind was bothering Harry, so that in the end the contentment of the one spilled over into the other.

"I've become a connoisseur of rest," said Harry, at last, as if John had asked the question. "Resting, dozing, half-sleep, slumber, sleep, deep sleep, unconsciousness. I think that's as far as it goes for now. When my brain has had enough of effort, it just selects from its menu of rest. It seems occupied with sorting things out for itself behind the scenes and does not want me bothering it all the time by reasoning or trying to remember. I like to think of my brain as a ruined city after an earthquake, with little figures climbing everywhere, digging in the wreckage, sorting through things and trying to put them back into some sort of order. Busy. Occasionally, they toss me a remnant and ask if it's what I'm looking for."

"Then I should leave you alone to rest."

"I am resting. I'm resting in company."

"I mean the effort of talking."

"Talking can be an effort. Not always. And listening isn't bad. After all, I don't have a past of my own to entertain me. I mean, listening can be bad, when there's too much going on, but I seem to be okay when there's a story. I like stories. You can tell me a story from your life if you feel like it. How you ended up living alone in that old farmhouse in New Hampshire, for example. And I see you watching Deva and Nadia, and that you are drawn to them, but you hold back. So, why alone, John? Don't worry if my eyes are closed." Harry resumed his stillness.

"Well," John said, "the short answer is that a long time ago my wife left me, and I never found anyone to take her place. She left me and took my two daughters with her."

He had never seen them again. They didn't want to see him, and he didn't try. They were grown up now—the daughters— with children of their own. He couldn't blame his wife. He'd deserved it, to be fair.

They had met as young, over-educated schoolteachers in a Brooklyn school long before Brooklyn was fashionable. Both had gone to good colleges—Georgetown for him, Wellesley for her—though he supposed this would not mean much to Harry. He would just say that both of them had received privileged educations earned on merit—and they had wanted to give something back, by doing something socially useful. It was the zeitgeist of the time. But in practice it had been hard, working in a rough neighborhood for poor salaries. They felt two of a kind, though she was from a prosperous family in Iowa, and he had grown up in Pennsylvania—in a nowhere industrial town where his father worked in a factory.

Well, they—he and Tania—married and three years later, at around the time that Tania became pregnant, John received a job offer from the State Department that promised a more practical future for a young family. A Georgetown schoolmate, already in place, made a convincing case that John's degree in international affairs belonged better inside the State Department than among the ungrateful poor of Brooklyn. It would be Washington at first, but overseas postings later if all went well. And a big difference in salary and prospects. There was, his friend pointed out, a world of the dispossessed to attend to. John didn't need to ferret them out in Brooklyn.

As it turned out, Tania hated living in Washington as a mother and wife, especially after John started to travel more, and was home with her less. He anticipated an overseas posting, but at first it was only short trips to embassies and consulates in between research and paperwork in DC. When their second daughter was born, Tania gave up the last remnant of her teaching career and for much of the time was also without the companionship of her husband. What had started out as a marriage of joint careers and joint vision was replaced by distance, made infuriatingly more distant by the burden of secrecy that came with his work. The State Department, Tania knew, was now only the official cover for his real government employer. She was inclined to think that the secrecy should not apply to her, as proof of his primary allegiance. She was not happy.

"And," John said, turning towards Harry, "I had an affair." Harry continued to breathe deeply and regularly, so that John did not know whether or not this had been heard. He decided to go on anyway. His job had become more active by that time and he was on mission a lot. The affair itself was nothing much. The work was stressful and finding himself lonely in a remote and unfriendly place he had taken advantage of an offer of comfort. With Tania's resentment at home, he supposed he had become vulnerable. It only happened once.

John paused, wondering where Harry was on his rest menu at this moment, and how much of what he was saying was being heard, and how deeply. And, if he was being understood, how was he being received. As he spoke, he heard his own elisions and wondered whether Harry could detect them too. If Harry did not know his own place in the world, what basis would he bring to moral judgment? Morality was, after all, mostly cultural. Harry never did seem to judge.

"I still loved Tania," John now asserted. "And, of course, I adored my two girls."

It was commonplace, this drifting apart. John saw it among his colleagues. He and Tania shared something early on, self-sacrifice, left-wing views, a sense of both mission and—to be honest—a sense of moral superiority. After Tania stopped working to stay at home with the children, these old principles came to mean more to her than to him. She hung on to her early left-wing identity and made herself unwelcome among the other Washington wives by being openly hostile towards

American foreign policy. It was easy for her in that way; she
didn't have to earn a living, or deal with the real world. John
felt that she despised him even though she never knew exactly what he did, or how difficult it was, and even though his
income supported her. In the end Tania had moved the family
out of Washington and back to her hometown in Iowa, where
her father was a banker lending to the surrounding farmers.
Her mother could offer relief with childcare, Tania argued, and
she might find some teaching work again. Houses were cheap
in Iowa farm towns and they bought a big, handsome one in
excellent condition, with wide porches, yellow paint, and the
shade of old trees. John kept a small apartment in DC.

"It was a restful place," John said to Harry, of the home in
Iowa.

Tania was more relaxed there, and became more welcoming
of John during his visits. When he told her that a longer overseas posting was is prospect—probably Pakistan, though he
really shouldn't say—and that they would be able to live together again as a proper family, Tania said that she wasn't sure.

Before Pakistan there was Brazil. It was the early eighties,
and he was given this small assignment, working alone. It was a
test of whether he had the right stuff before being given more
authority. He explained to Tania, hoping for approval, that he
had been seconded to a development aid project, concerned
with helping settlers and indigenous peoples on the edge of the
Amazon. That was his official cover. But it had been a rough,
lonely, disquieting assignment and he returned to Iowa feeling
dirty and self-disgusted. It was the early eighties, still the time of
the generals and America's support for them at any cost. Someone had spat in his face. The company he had been obliged
to keep had been unsavory, and he had been almost forced by
local custom to choose a woman. His local counterparts had
more or less insisted that he did so as proof that he accepted
them, their people and their ways, and was a man to be trusted,
and indeed that he was a man at all. And so there had been the

girl, making the best out of necessity. This is what he told the silent, sleeping Harry.

On his return, exhausted and demoralized, Tania had looked hard at John. When he talked blandly about the project, she knew she was not getting the whole truth. He was thin when he arrived home and he spent his first days lodged in his favorite spot, the porch swing seat, sipping whiskey to relax. He was skittish with the girls, at first clasping them to him too strongly, and then fending off their playfulness, as if uncomfortable with too much touch. He had seen Tania sense this self-disgust in him and he wanted to blurt out everything so that she would understand how difficult things were, and sympathize. He wanted her to understand that deep inside he was still the same decent man she had loved in Brooklyn, so that she would comfort him. He wanted her blessing.

In the event, Tania had gone for him, taking politics as her weapon. What was he doing in Latin America working for the vile military dictatorships that American foreign policy was shamefully supporting? How could he live with himself working for generals and their thugs, the militias and death squads and the like, America's shameful Cold War allies? How could she even live with him?

John had mounted a weak defense: you worked with what you had, within the constraints; you did your job; he didn't make American foreign policy; you couldn't stop being involved in countries simply because you didn't like their current governments—there weren't any governments left to like; the new generals in Brazil were not as bad as the old ones. And where in the world would she have him work? Cuba? China? The Soviet Union? You did your best with what there was, and tried to prevent something worse. You stayed engaged and took the long view. That was the real world. She was happy enough to live in a comfortable, secure America, wasn't she? He couldn't afford her cheap emotions. He heard himself saying these things, and heard a stranger.

They had been clearing dishes from the kitchen table to the sink, but now they came to be standing toe to toe, while the girls were still sitting at the table staring silently at their plates, scared by the unprecedented surge of anger coursing between their parents, this unprecedented tipping over of self-control. "Cheap emotions." That did it. Tania's face went pink with anger both at what she knew and at what she suspected would anger her if she knew more. Of course, there must have been easy women along with the corruption and violence. They went together. And why would he stop at one transgression? She could sense his guilt. Cheap emotions—from the man who had cheapened theirs. She told him that he had sold out and was not the man she married. Instead of saving the poor, he was working for the oppressors of the poor, the murderers of the poor. He told her that she did not know what she was talking about, but she brushed that aside with a sweep of her hand. And could he, she asked, look her in the eye, and tell her that he'd been faithful to her? He couldn't, could he? Did he think she did not know it, with her cheap emotions?

He hadn't answered. There had been the girl. He'd settle for infidelity and for taking his punishment before a more damning charge might be brought, the one that was silencing him, the girl's voice, Veronica's voice: "You rape me." Tania was repeating, "I'm not wrong. I'm not wrong," and started slapping his face with her open palm, little slaps, gaining force while he stayed still and silent. "Deny it!" she said, and when he did not, she pummeled at his chest, tears flowing. She had screamed, "You disgust me," and "I'm alone. Alone in fucking Iowa because of you," although, objectively, he was the one more alone. Her blows accumulated, beginning to hurt and do damage. She scrabbled at his chest with her hands and nails as if trying to excavate him, to find the man she loved hidden inside. He tried to hold her wrists to stop her, then looked over at his horrified daughters, six and eight, and tried to smile at them, as if all this stuff going on between the grown-ups was really not a serious thing. It did not occur to him to walk away; he was standing his ground, and with Tania's renewed, hysterical attack, taking his punishment. But then it was suddenly all too much, all the violence he had seen and absorbed, the deaths, the girl spitting in his face, everything. This had to stop now. Stop now! He hit Tania in the face. In between launching the blow and the blow landing, his arm had picked up anger from the air, and his hand had made a fist, so that the punch surprised him with its force. It was square and hard with all of a man's strength behind it, and no restraint.

Tania staggered back but did not fall. John had created silence. She was not falling because she was desperate that the children should not see her fall, that they should not forever remember their father punching their mother and their mother falling. He could see she was fighting for consciousness, but he was frozen to the spot. Her face had turned entirely white. During this moment of whiteness John thought that miraculously he had done no damage. Then the blood broke out from the whiteness, from a deeply cut lip, from a smashed nose, a split cheek. Blood sprung out, joyful with the surprise of its liberation. It bloomed across her face and overflowed onto the floor. John stood there, stunned. He understood too late that Tania's blows had been communication, but that his had been destruction. She gave up on the battle for her dignity and fell to all fours, blood pooling at his feet, then she laboriously turned and crawled away across the gray kitchen tiles, leaving a trail of bright red spots. She looked over her shoulder once, in fear, in case he had not finished. At the back door she pulled herself up by the door handle and, turning to the girls, gargled through the blood, "Car!" They had followed her obediently to the bronze Camry parked in the driveway outside the door. The younger one, Beatrice, had stopped in the doorway to look back at him with huge, shocked eyes, willing him still to be the beloved father who could put things right. He shook his head very slightly, and Tania had called out, "Beatrice! Now!"

The last he saw of them was the red flash of brake lights at the intersection of Walnut and Vine. The trail of bright red led back to him, along the driveway, across the kitchen floor, to the pool at his feet. Later that day, he received a call from Tania's father offering him the police or his immediate departure never to be seen again. He chose departure. The youngest, Beatrice, would be over forty now.

John concluded his account with, "It's what I saw again, when I came to, after that blank episode with the daffodils: the instant when my wife's blood broke out from her white face. One of the things I saw. One of the horrors. Anyway, it's why I live alone, I suppose. The long version. I'm unfit for human companionship. I've been busy not remembering for half a lifetime, which means, I suppose, busy not having in my life anything that might remind me of it. Love, for example." John gave a little choked laugh, then looked over at Harry whose face was unchanged. He watched for a moment, then whispered, "Harry, I hope you're sleeping."

"No," said Harry. "Not really."

"Then I'm wondering, will you be asking me to leave?"

Harry stayed silent, his breaths coming evenly while John held his. At last, he said, "No, of course not. At this moment, I feel like I'm you. It would be like asking myself to leave. You know, John, I don't know a thing about my past. I may have done terrible things. I probably did. I just don't know. So, I would be foolish to judge you, wouldn't I?" He opened his eyes and turned his head towards John, some small mischief in the look.

John said, "I may have done worse things too."

"It doesn't matter."

"I've tried hard to forget."

"You see," said Harry. "There I have the advantage. I find it hard to remember."

"I'm sorry…"

"No, it's not a problem. You're trying to forget and I'm trying to remember. And we're both failures at it. Perhaps it's in the trying that we're going wrong."

"Perhaps," said John. "It doesn't seem to be working for me. Not anymore."

"John, it makes everyone happy to have you here. We all like you. Deva, Nadia, me. We all want your company. Then has nothing to do with now."

His instinct—John's—was to argue with this assessment and deny there could be reasons for anyone to want him, but he stopped himself. When was the last time someone had said they wanted him? He couldn't remember. He decided to let the moment stand.

M orning, John," said Dr Elliot. "Settled in?"
"I think so."
"No problems?"
"They've both been very welcoming."

"Good. And do you recognize Harry? Is he who we think he is?"

"My friend's son? I don't know. He could be. He could be a Pakistani from North West Frontier who's spent most of his life in Europe. He's cosmopolitan in his manner. Well educated, obviously. His culture is mostly English. At least superficially. The father didn't have his green eyes. But there are green-eyed people in that part of Pakistan. So, he could be Pakistani, but he could just as well be something else."

"You don't actually recognize him."

"I saw the son once in a crowd of people when he was about twelve, so, no. It's hard to match the face with the father. The father was a tough, bearded tribal leader who spent his days outside on a horse and always wore something on his head. Harry seems to have led a cultured, comfortable life in England. And is clean shaven."

"And the memory loss. What's your reading on that? Is he faking it?"

"I think it's genuine."

"But we know it's not stable. It's already changed since Deva arrived. He could be managing it."

"I don't think he remembers anything of his past life."

"You sound very confident."

"That's my take. It's hard to say exactly why. It's something to do with how open he seems. And what a good listener he is. It's like he's full of space."

"Full of space?" Dr Elliot mused, mockingly. "Well, hardly

a medical diagnosis, John. Or even a professional analysis. But we'll leave it for now. How does he react to you? Any sort of recognition there, do you think? Suspicion? He knew your name, after all."

"Nothing, as far as I can tell. He's kind."

"Kind?"

"Yes, actually."

"Well, we need progress. This all costs money and manpower. And we still don't know the nature of the threat, or who else is involved. Do you have ideas on how to proceed? Does he seem fragile?"

"He doesn't seem fragile. But I think he may be fragile."

"You're sounding as if you like him. But I assume you are more professional than that. Even if you are a bit rusty. Let me make it clear. We're talking about terrorism here, John. Imminent threat. Your fragile, kind man met with the ISS before leaving Pakistan. He has motive. He hid out in Lebanon. With arms dealers. He came to your house and you didn't spot him. He was up to something and we need to find out what. This is about how we can crack open a memory without cracking him. Is the girl helping?"

"She got me here. She keeps him relaxed."

"But now what?"

"I'm still feeling my way. He's coming to trust me."

"Which is why you fed him all that personal stuff? Is any of that true, by the way?"

"Why lie, when the truth serves better? Harry is supersensitive. He can sense bullshit. He's never going to open up to you, by the way. And he doesn't trust Mrs. Slater's friendliness either. You two are going to get nowhere. He thinks you are unloving people with closed hearts, and he feels sorry for you. But he trusts Deva absolutely. And he's coming to trust me, I think. It takes time."

"Which we don't have. You'll let me know the first time you have any inkling of an opening in his forgetting?"

"That is my assignment, I believe."

"And meanwhile, start to make use of that trust that's costing us so much. Push him a bit. He owes you some confidences."

"Right."

"I'll see you again in a few days?"

"As you wish." John stood and turned to leave.

"John," said Dr Elliot, "do you have direct contact with your own people?"

"No."

"But I don't suppose you'd tell me if you did, would you?"

"It would depend."

"Well, this is our show. You're our guest. You're under our protection. We're supposed to be cooperating. The best of friends, of course."

"Of course."

"Deva," asked John, "where do you think Harry is from?"

Nadia was already in bed, and Harry had returned, as he did each evening, to a long night of healing sleep, his brain casting about for its lost instruments of memory. Deva and John were sitting on the couch, relaxed, Deva with herbal tea, John a whiskey. It was John's opportunity to drink, since Harry didn't. Harry's reasons for it—medical, ethical, religious, or taste—were unclear but definite enough to discourage John from taking a whiskey in his company. He had asked Deva whether his drinking would bother her, and she replied, "John, I sing in a nightclub." Then, "I don't drink now because I used to drink too much. Now I don't need to. But you should if you want. In your case I might even prescribe it."

Now Deva said, apropos of Harry's origins, "I'm not sure."

"But not Brazil?"

"Definitely not Brazil."

"Why not?"

"Well, it's true we come in all shades. From his looks alone, I think I wouldn't be able to say. It's in the way he moves, his manner, his eye contact—little things that add up. And the way he talks. Not just the language—he doesn't use his hands and body the way we do. Have you noticed his English is perfectly English? You know, it's nuanced, up to date, specifically London. And in the background, it's educated. He may have been born here. Or at least he must have lived here a long time. But obviously there's something else as well."

"What is that? You're the anthropologist."

"I don't know—a formality of some kind. Okay, there's an assumption of physical separateness that isn't Latin American. Or African, for that matter. But it's not English reserve. It's not uncomfortable at all—he's fine with touch. It's gentle and respectful. You feel close, but never invaded. Do you feel the same, as a man, or is it just me?"

"There is something like that."

"Maybe a Middle-eastern parent. Or Asian. Maybe a mixture. Some Euro—Italian or French—and something else. The French have that formality—at least I think the richer ones do."

"A French colony?"

"I don't know. Algeria? Lebanon had a lot of French influence, I think. The Lebanese are cosmopolitan."

"But does he ever speak French?"

"No. Only English. Do you know what Mrs. Slater told me? That she thought that Harry was really spelled Hari, with an *i* on the end, and was short for Haruki. Japanese. Then she backed off and said she could be wrong. I don't trust her. I can't see any Japanese in him, can you? What did Dr Elliot tell you?"

"That they had open mind."

"He told me the same. And that I mustn't pollute his memory," said Deva wryly.

"You like him, Deva, don't you?"

"Harry? Of course. Very much. He never complains. He's good hearted. Generous. Nice to look at. Dresses well. Do you notice how he always turns things around so you end up talking about yourself? It's amazing, given what he's gone through. To be so concerned about others. But I feel comfortable with him. I think he likes me, but he never assumes anything. I like it—unless of course it's because I'm losing it."

"It?"

"My irresistibility."

"Ah."

"He doesn't have that needy thing that most men have."

"Let me reassure you, Deva," said John. "You haven't lost it." And so saying, he dropped his eyes and paid attention to his drink.

"Thank you, John." Deva curled her legs under herself and tugged down at her skirt.

John noted that, as always, her blouse was undone the extra button. This was just Deva. Now she did something with her hair, piling it up and letting it fall, then stretching, an action that pushed her breasts against her blouse. This was how she was, always radiating a few degrees of extra heat. John reminded himself that it was just Deva, and that none of it was aimed at him.

Relaxed now, Deva said, "You know, John, I do find something attractive about Harry. It's not sexual. A simplicity."

"Maybe if you lose your memory, you lose some complexity too," John replied, his mind not completely on the subject. He had not been this close to a woman for many years. Decades. Not since his marriage, really. Not like this: an evening drink, easy talk, low lights, the twinkling city, smooth skin a hand's width away. Deva was relaxed, he thought, because she did not count him as a threatening man, and he determined that he would treasure this. When Deva unwound herself and stretched, her hair came close enough for him to smell, which he did, breathing it in. He was like a man released from prison. The scent of a woman's hair. He had forgotten. He loved the scent of Deva. He was going soft.

"There was something once," Deva mused. "Once, early on, Harry might have spoken in another language. He was half asleep. Then he continued in English as if he had been speaking it all along. It wasn't anything I recognized. Maybe it was just some nonsense his brain threw out. I didn't tell Elliot."

"Not Arabic."

"I'd recognize Arabic."

"Farsi?"

"That too. Or at least it would have sounded familiar. I have Iranian friends."

"Urdu? Moving east."

"I don't know Urdu."

"It has some Farsi in it," said John, but didn't press, asking instead, "What about his accident? Do you know much about that?"

"The car crash? Not much. But I know he was driving a Porsche. He said it was his brother's. A stupid car. And when he drove me home the night before, he wasn't a very confident driver. But he was careful. Slow. You know, I hadn't thought of that until now. He mentioned a brother that first night—he said a brother owned the car. But they've told me there is no family. I wonder if he made it up."

"They know more than they're telling us. This keeping us in the dark so we don't pollute his memory with the facts stuff—I'm not sure I buy it."

"I wish they would tell us everything they know," said Deva. "Then maybe we could help him more. You know he's convinced you can help him? Can you?"

"Only if believing that helps him. I really don't know how to help him."

"Nothing from all your travels helping poor foreigners?"

"Well, I met a lot of people. I might not remember."

"John, are you sure you weren't a spy?" Deva twisted around to look at him.

"That's such a media thing, isn't it? People imagine that anyone who works internationally is a spy because that's what they see all the time on TV. Or in films. But most people working internationally, are just working. There are millions of us—governments, corporations, the UN, all sorts of international agencies, non-governmental organizations. Nothing glamorous. You know that. You're an anthropologist. You're one of them."

"So, who did you work for?"

"American government aid to begin with. USAID. Then I was freelance, working with various agencies. I specialized in disasters. Relieving them, you know, not making them. Making disasters would be more my personal life. If I wrote a memoir, I could call it, *The Disaster Specialist.* I started accidentally with an earthquake in Pakistan and then got a reputation. It's how careers happen."

"How about Pakistani. For Harry. Lots of them in England. Though he's not that dark?"

"In parts of Pakistan they aren't dark. They can look European. Even blond. Once I spent an hour thinking I was talking to a Danish aid expert and he turned out to be the Pakistani deputy commissioner. He was very polite about my mistake, but I was left desperately trying to remember what I'd said about the Pakistan government."

"Brazil too. We have our blonds."

"Something going back to Alexander the Great coming along the Silk Road, I heard. For Pakistan, I mean."

Deva had stopped looking at John and was slumped back on the couch. Something had contaminated the mood. John supposed it might be the subtle influence of his dissembling. He looked to regain intimacy and steered the conversation towards something intimate that he might confess. "Were you ever married, Deva?" he asked.

"No. Men were like drinks. I could never stop at just one." She laughed, then said, "Except for Nadia's father, and he died."

"I'm sorry."

"We were never married. It never even occurred to us."

"I was married. Then I behaved badly and lost my wife and both daughters forever. Deserved it. I sort of gave up then. For the sake of the others. I told Harry all about it the other day. First time I've talked about it in decades." He offered Deva a grim little smile.

Deva swiveled her whole body around to face him. "John, you know, I think you need to get over your own story. You always talk like everything's in the past for you. You're not that old. You needn't be old unless you want to be. We thought you were an old man from the photo, but you're not. You need to cheer up, dance, find a woman and, you know, do her. I don't mean me, but someone. I think you've given up. I can see it on your face. I look at you and think, There's someone who's locked himself up and thrown away the key. I can see the prison bars. It makes me angry to see someone not even try at life. So, you messed up one marriage. Ages ago. Some people have messed up five marriages. You need some life. You need Brazil.

I'm going to take you to the Miranda with me. I'm going to make you dance with Brazilians."

Deva stood up as if she was going to take him dancing right now. John stared up at her, speechless.

"Never mind," she said. "What do I care if you want to die before you're dead. In any case, it's time for sleep. Good night, John Bradley." She stood, straightened her clothes, and headed briskly towards her room while John tracked her exit. She was barely out of sight before she stalked back in, planted a kiss on John's forehead, and stalked back out again, trailing, "Some people don't even get a chance at life. Some don't even live long enough. You have to fight. I've had to fight. Oh, and one more thing, you've got lipstick on your head."

On the night when Harry went to find Deva at the Miranda, driving his late brother's Porsche, he became stuck in traffic outside Kensington High Street Tube station, and fell to looking for himself in the street. He was not the man in a suit driving a silver car that caught the attention of passersby. Rather, he was a man in jeans taking the station steps two at a time, then tacking through the crowd, an inconspicuous man, part of the scene, more watching than watched, a notebook and pen ready in his jacket pocket, a man walking free in London, a Londoner, his mind unbound. Happy, he now knew.

At the end of his days—involving whatever café conversations, meetings, films, or bookshop readings—that man had returned on the Tube to Tufnell Park, to a shared house of people much like himself: single, educated, thirties, up to interesting things. There was a journalist from Romania, a German documentary filmmaker, a college lecturer in English literature, a new American girl who was trying to make a living from an arts blog below the immigration radar, and there was the older woman who owned the handsome house and had made a community of it for her own satisfaction. And there was him, the Pakistani poet from a wealthy family, who hadn't been back to Pakistan since he was sent to school in England over twenty years before. Nobody really thought of him as Pakistani any more.

While Harry was in a Porsche in a traffic jam, those people, his housemates, were probably sitting around the enormous kitchen table, half busy, half chatting, half eating, half on their way out of the door. They would still be expecting him back. People were always traveling unpredictably and an absence raised few questions. His room was still there, he supposed, insulated against everything by books from floor to ceiling. For a moment he thought of abandoning the car by the side of the road and just going home to his old life. Instead, he was going to a nightclub—more his brother's scene—and then back to the same brother's extravagant home off Baker Street—well, the family's London home really, though in practice mainly the home of his brother, as the manager of their international business interests. It was ridiculously big, and now uncomfortably empty. He was living in his brother's house, driving his brother's car, wearing his brother's suit, even his shoes.

Everyone called him Harry, which he signed as Hari, even though papers did occasionally still arrive addressed to Zamir Afridi. The new name started as a sort of joke when he was nineteen and his first poem was accepted by a literary magazine. In his callowness, he decided he needed a pen name that more reflected the global citizenship to which he aspired, and although the magazine editor had at first resisted losing his Pakistani poet, he ended up reconciled to publishing the mysteriously exotic Haruki Chateaubriand.

That name had been cooked up in a pub with friends at the University of East Anglia, and he had since regretted its juvenile pretension. But as he became a little known as a poet, then better established, there was no turning back without orphaning his early work. And, in all honesty, the name had succeeded in freeing him from his origins, and had set him apart in his career, creating a little buzz of extra interest. It was an amalgam of two writers who happened to influence him at the time: Francois Rene de Chateaubriand the father of Romanticism, and Haruki Murakami, whose novels of magical ordinariness he had then just discovered.

He no longer had much contact with the family back in Pakistan, except for his beloved sister Samina, and in particular he had no contact with the family business. Indeed, he had little contact with the older brother living a few miles away in London. That his ability to live as a poet depended in large part on money from the family was an embarrassment, and his reason for living simply was to reduce the size of this embarrassment. He was the youngest son of three, and his father had never criticized his choice of career. The Afridis belonged to a culture with an ancient respect for poetry. His wish to stay in England was never much resisted.

Harry's single book of collected poems was well received by its three print reviewers. The excellent *Times Literary Supplement* review characterized him as a new sort of nature poet, for whom London and Londoners were taken to be nature, a poet whose outsider status was gained from his belonging nowhere and everywhere, yet who seemed intimately conversant with the idioms of English and its poetic traditions. He was in short, a "Martian Romantic." It was a very good review quote and the book did well for a poetry book. That is, its sales were in the high hundreds. With its publication, he felt that he had made a road in life.

Now, in Kensington High Street, the traffic ahead of him had moved on. Someone hooted from behind and for a moment he panicked, forgetting how to drive the car. He had never owned a car in London. He once had a license but had long ago mislaid it. This car was a fancy sort of automatic; he only had to press the accelerator. When he did so, it leapt forward and he braked fiercely so as not to pounce on a little red car stopped in front of him. People turned in his direction. He knew what they were thinking: a ridiculous rich foreigner in an expensive car that he couldn't even drive. It was what he would have thought.

Harry remembered none of this.

D eva said matter-of-factly, working on her own nails, "Ask Harry. I'm busy," and Nadia went to where Harry sat on the couch, carrying the little curved nail scissors with her. She sat next to him, offered the scissors, and said, "Help me, Harry. I can't do this. I started, but it's difficult." She held out a small hand on which the miniature nails had some time ago been painted blue and were now chipped blue above pink, above tiny pale half-moons. "You've got nothing to do," Nadia pointed out.

Harry turned to her from the state of reverie that filled most of his new, continuously remembered life. It was a state lit by his enjoyment of this home with these other people in it, their things, their mess, their sounds and smells. When he woke in the mornings it was to these facts that his mind raced, relieved first to find them still in his mind, and relieved a second time to find them outside his door. He was in possession of a life, and was not alone in this strange world. This tenderness he felt—the instinctive knowledge of Deva and Nadia's feelings, and now John's, and the wish to helpfully act on this knowledge—was, according to Deva, love. He knew that the John of the photo had lived without love, and therefore had been unhappy. Harry wanted everyone, especially John, to know happiness.

Nadia and Deva's move into the house had been Harry's idea. When he first thought of it, after a few weeks of Deva's daily visits, the idea seemed so obvious that he berated himself for the dreamy stupidity that had prevented him from thinking of it earlier. Each day, Deva arrived late and left early because she had a daughter, Nadia. She could not stay overnight, even though the house was so large, because she had Nadia. The obvious solution was to invite both of them to live with him. When he told Mrs. Slater of his brilliant idea, she said she would have to consult Dr Elliot. She wondered aloud if Harry might not find it too much to have two people around all the time, especially the uncontrollable energy of a child. And she reported back that Dr Elliot did not think it was a good idea—could see no utility in it.

Harry, with exceptional independence, asked Deva to bring Nadia for a visit, and Nadia had done her work. Her entry hand in hand with Deva, a miniature of the original down to dimples and fashion sense, lifted a spirit inside Harry, an absolute certainty that this little being could do him only good.

Nadia, on her arrival, had seen a big, light space with very little of interest in it. There was a man, but no children, nothing colored, nothing to play with, nothing happening. The responsibility on her shoulders to transform this emptiness into fun pressed on her. The man had offered his hand, and she'd liked him. When Deva sat at one end of the long couch and Harry at the other, Nadia claimed the middle. A woman who did not smile brought in drinks and biscuits—orange juice for her, without even asking for her preference. While the grown-ups talked above her, Nadia discovered that if she lay down on the couch with her head just touching her mother's thigh, her stockinged feet exactly reached Harry's leg, making a connection. He seemed not to notice this until just as Nadia reached to scratch her itchy foot, he took it in his hand and pressed the very spot. It didn't tickle, but seemed like it could have done, so Nadia giggled and wriggled anyway, until finally she detached Harry's attention from her mother, and won a smile, and some action, while Deva just shook her head.

Nadia pulled her feet away, then let Harry catch them, then repeated, and when she judged that freedom of movement was fully sanctioned, she stood on the couch and bounced a little, holding on to Harry's shoulder for balance, though she might have chosen Deva's. For Harry, this dependent touch of a small person was all joyful discovery. Deva and Nadia, he decided, absolutely must move in.

Connection established and permission assumed, Nadia

began to find larger possibilities in the room. She went to the wall of glass, and was only briefly caught by the view through it, before the effects of her breath on it became more interesting. The rhythm of misting and vanishing—now you see it, now you don't—put all of London within her power. Then there was also the discovery of the shiny wood floor, the sheer extent of it, the going to the middle and twirling around with arms outstretched that it invited. Harry said, "I did that too. You can slide if you're careful." He kicked off his shoes to modestly demonstrate, winning arched eyebrows from Deva. Nadia did slide a little in imitation, rather cautious, before demanding, "Look!"—the instruction specifically directed at Harry—and executed a movement from her ballet class, extending her arms and dipping and spinning, ending with tangled legs and an embarrassed, "I got it wrong," to Harry, followed by a string of Portuguese explication to Deva.

Harry said, "I couldn't begin to do that. I can only slide a bit."

"I could teach you," said Nadia, but at this, Deva, feeling that Nadia's aspiration to command all attention was sufficiently indulged, and mindful of Dr Elliot's strict instruction to make the visit short, had said, "Another day. We have to go."

"Certainly, another day," agreed Harry.

On the next day he proposed that they should move in. It would be better for him, better for everyone. There was all this space to fill.

When Dr Elliot expressed his continuing reservations, Harry found authority, and insisted.

Now Harry thought that Nadia bringing her scissors to him, and placing her tiny, rubbery fingers in his hand, was even better than her teaching him to dance. He said, "Let me see," and took her small hand in his. So fragile, and in his charge.

"I did this one," said Nadia, wagging a finger with a jagged nail, "but it's sharp."

He took the finger with due seriousness and carefully trimmed the jag, checking for smoothness with his fingertip.

Nadia imitated the test, announcing, "Good," and offering her other fingers. "Short, please," she said.

The angle of approach, sitting side by side, was awkward, a problem solved by Nadia climbing onto his lap, showing him the way it should be done, her back to him, his arms encircling her. She turned to give him the quick smile that signaled, in both mother and daughter, irresistible intent. Harry navigated the little curved scissors around Nadia's nails, fearful at being so close to the quick, and at having been offered so much confidence in his ability to not cause pain. She nestled against him, settled between his chest and thighs, fenced in by his arms, sharing his concentration on her fingers. Her bottom was bony, her hair smelled sweet, her trust was an ocean. This was the richest life Harry had known in his short new life. This was human and astonishing.

Nadia regarded her nails and was satisfied, saying, "Thanks, Harry." She hopped off his lap and was on to the next thing, joining and unjoining with matter-of-fact ease.

"Thanks, Harry," echoed Deva, waving her separated fingers in the air, drying the nail polish.

Some weeks later, after John arrived and was settled in his room, Deva said to Harry, without warning, "I have to go to the shops. Women's business. Can you keep an eye on Nadia?" It was not a question really, since Deva was halfway through the door when she asked, and was fully through before Harry could react to this new thing: responsibility.

Nadia gave no sign of being perturbed. Her playthings were spread across the floor, among them two plastic dolls' houses with walls and roofs that could be arranged and rearranged, along with the furnishings inside and trees outside, the people an inch tall, the animals to scale. She was absorbed in these houses, chattering in a mixture of English and Portuguese, affecting not to notice either her mother's departure or the novel arrangement of her being in the charge of Harry, along with the opportunity to claim him entirely as her own. At last, she flashed him a smile, completely confident that she would find him paying attention.

"Do you need anything?" Harry asked. Should he ask Mrs. Slater to bring her a drink?

Nadia shook her head and frowned at this irrelevance, then sighed theatrically, "I don't know why this fence will not stand up," and she demonstrated how the garden fence would not plug in with her push, but toppled sideways.

Harry went to kneel by her, unconcerned with creasing his trousers. He had nothing to do with the routine laundering of his clothes. "Hold that," instructed Nadia. "No, not like that. Over here, so I can join it with the house." He bent lower to better see the detail, then lay down on his stomach like Nadia was lying on hers, entering her world of play.

"Good," said Nadia. "This is Serena's house. She lives with her mother and father and her little brother, Ming."

"Ming?"

"Yes, Ming's from China. Serena's parents adopted him, but Serena loves him too. Serena's American."

"They live in America?"

"Yes, like my father."

"He's American, your father?"

"Of course. But he died. I never met him." She glanced up to see how Harry was taking this, and noting that he simply took it, she turned back to her game and rattled on. "No...that's not right, they live in Brazil. Serena's mother is from Brazil."

"And who lives in the house next door?"

"Serena's best friend. But she's not allowed to play with Serena because her father is rich and he only wants her to play with rich children."

"What's her friend's name?"

"Fatima. But they don't care what their fathers think because they are best friends, so they've made a secret hole here. See?" Nadia poked her little finger through the secret hole in the fence. "And Fatima climbs out of her window and down the tree so she can visit Serena. Like this."

Harry fell into Nadia's imagined world, and put forward a few of his own ideas about the histories of Serena, Fatima, and Ming, enjoying this, the inventing of pasts.

"I'm coming to dinner," he said on Ming's behalf. "Do you have my favorite food?"

Nadia considered this. "What is your favorite food? We may not have it."

"Chocolate."

"No, Ming. You know you can't have chocolate for dinner. You have to have salad."

Ming was still making the case for chocolate over salad when Harry looked up to see John standing at the door, taking in the scene. He seemed to have been watching for a while. "You can join us," said Harry to John, then, "Don't you think?" deferring to Nadia. She considered this, not sure that anyone else was required, before conceding that, "John could be Serena's papai. He's coming home from work."

"What do you think, John, could you be Serena's papai? He's a nice man, isn't he, Nadia?"

"Oh yes," she confirmed. "But he's strict."

John smiled faintly, but found he could not move across the room into the land of play. He had played with his daughters, long ago, and it was the memory of this that had stopped him in the doorway and kept him there. He did not think he ever could do it again. He shook his head. "No, I'll leave you to carry on. You look happy. The floor is a long way down for me." He turned to return to his room, so that Harry returned to Nadia and Ming, making a mental note of John's regret.

When Deva returned, Nadia and Harry did not at first notice her. Both pleased and miffed by their inattention, Deva crept close, so that when Harry did look up, there was the shock of a leg and a body to traverse before his view could reach her face. Her breasts were shaking, which proved to be because she was laughing silently.

"So, has Nadia been entertaining you?" Deva enquired.

There was the delightful unlikely rightness of it, Harry and her daughter lost together in a single world, playing at her feet.

"Harry's fun!" asserted Nadia.

With some reluctance Harry pushed himself up to sit on his heels. "Nadia's very cruel," he said. "She wouldn't give Ming chocolate for dinner."

"Well, good! She's right. Ming is a bad influence. Now, Nadia, go and wash. It's nearly time to eat." Then, "Why do we always have to wait for Mrs. Slater to cook dinner? I can cook. Would you like to try something different, Harry?"

He thought. "I don't know. I think we eat well, don't we?"

"Yes, but isn't there anything in particular you'd like that I could make for you?" She waited, in case the reply offered a clue to Harry's past.

He said, "I don't know. I can't think of anything." He sounded humble and a little lost. From where she stood, Deva could reach down to where Harry kneeled and touch his head, and she found this irresistible, placing her palm on his crown, on his brain, and leaving it there, as if all that was damaged inside might be mended by her touch. Harry did not move, listening to the message of Deva's palm.

When she removed her hand, Deva said, "Oh, sorry, I forgot. The perfect hair," and she mussed it with her departing fingers.

"That's okay," he said, "it felt good," leading Nadia to spring up and ruffle it into fuller messiness.

"No, that's too much, Nadia," said Deva.

"He said it was okay."

"It is okay," confirmed Harry, and mussed Nadia's in return until she giggled helplessly with the mutual mussing, and Deva left them to it, heading for the bathroom, saying, "Do I have two children now?"

In Rio, in 1991, if you looked like Veronica, you could not but turn a thousand heads. In appearance, Veronica and Deva, both pretty, were obviously from the same mold, except that the mother always looked down against attention, while the daughter looked up into it. For some men demureness was an invitation to possess, but Deva's mother found none of these suitors worthy of auditioning for the role of adorer, or protector. Veronica had something else in mind. Little Deva liked to think this was love for her absent father.

Deva confided this to Harry, their conversation over weeks having moved from the absence of Nadia's father to the absence of her own. Deva speculated that the former absence might be in some way a consequence of the latter. Harry listened while Deva threw her life into the dark well of him.

She came to the part of her story of which she had never spoken and which she had spent a lifetime not remembering. Alcohol had helped her in this, and sex had also helped. But it had been heroin that had proved the most effective in this long project of forgetting.

Deva had decided, when she was eight or nine, that her mother needed a husband. She could not say how much of this was on her own account to avoid the taunts of schoolmates, and how much was because she saw her mother struggling alone to make a life for them. Or, perhaps, it was just that there was a total absence of men in her life and she was curious about them. Or, perhaps, she had felt in some unarticulated way that they were too close, the mother and child, and that the mother's love and pride assigned too weighty a responsibility to the child. In any case, by the time she was nine or ten, and her mother was all of twenty-six, Deva took it upon herself to match-make, embarrassing her mother by asking promising men whether they did not think her mother was beautiful and informing them that she was single.

In retrospect, Deva could imagine that her mother might have been calculating that by her thirties she would be free of Deva and in a position to start a whole new life while still relatively young. There was a discontinued education to continue, and the prospect of finding a man on her own level, the level of her educated father, a husband who could then choose her, Veronica, without the complication of also choosing a child. But as that child, Deva could not conceive of life as stages, nor imagine any advantage for her mother in being free of her. It seemed to Deva that her mother would never find a husband if she continued to be so passive and to live so much in the past.

Deva set herself at Manuel, who fixed their wiring and unclogged their pipes, and did so for free, a man both useful and kind, who Deva noted was invited to sit at the kitchen table for coffee once his work was done, and who made her mother laugh. Deva flirted with him, and him with her, while her mother smiled at this funny sweetness, understanding that the flirting with her daughter was a proxy for flirting with her, an indirect testing of the waters on Manuel's part, and also a signaling that he was not put off by the existence of a child. On Deva's part, her childish signaling signified her wish for a fuller family, and that Manuel might do.

He was older than Veronica, in his mid-thirties, the same age as her father when he died. Importantly for Deva at the time, he was the typical age of her schoolmates' fathers. Manuel was always loathe to leave the kitchen table and prolonged his visits with stories about his job at the "Light," the city's electric utility, pretending to Deva that he personally pedaled the bicycle that powered the city's electricity. He invited her to test the proof of it by pressing his thigh muscles—and explained that the power cuts were when he, or one of his fellows, took a break to go to the toilet, or just became too tired to carry on. His cycling home from their house to his late at night was the final straw in his exhaustion, he claimed, and if only he could stay, the reliability of Rio's power would be much improved the following day. "Can't he?" Deva pleaded. "Can't Manuel stay?"

This must have worked, Deva thought, the way she chatted and brightened when Manuel was around, because he eventually did stay. She walked into her mother's section of the room one morning, bleary-eyed—at the time Deva had only recently acquired her own mattress, and only recently had a pink cotton sheet been hung across the room to give each of them some slight separation—to find Manuel looking back at her, alone in her mother's bed, the sound of splashing water coming from the bathroom. On the pillow, his beard was darker than the night before, and therefore his smile more white. Under his face was a chest as coarsely hairy as a mat. Deva pushed into the bathroom and announced, delightedly—though her news could not have been news—"Mamie, Manuel is in your bed!" Her mother had straightened from where she was bent over the sink and gave Deva's delight a long, considering look, before making a little noise between surprise and relief, then saying. "So, Deva, when Manuel is here, you will have to be more modest. Bring your clothes to the bathroom when you get dressed."

In the end, Manuel moved in, his small but regular salary from the Light improving the family's diet and clothes, and Deva's status at her school. Sometimes larger items appeared, a TV and a stereo, which much later Deva came to understand were the fruits of the bribes that Manuel received for favoring particular customers of the utility.

Arguments were another innovation in the household, though arguments with Deva's mother were lopsided affairs. Manuel blustered and Veronica simply did nothing in response. In this passivity, Deva now said, she did not take after her mother, who seemed not to be affected by Manuel's bluster, but simply continued to be her self-contained self, not offering competing points of view or any justifications. On such occasions Veronica seemed to become more complete, more poised, as if quite accepting that Manuel's anger existed, and this might, in the way of the world, be normal and understandable, but not accepting that any reaction to the anger was necessary. Her proper response, she seemed to feel, was to listen but to remain entirely unaffected. Fighting was ludicrous; there was little she wanted from the world, and what she wanted was mainly to be found within herself. This aspect of Veronica at first enchanted Manuel, but later infuriated him. He was not an exceptional man, or even a particularly good man. It emerged that he was habitually corrupt. He was just an ordinary man, who had, as he saw it, taken on a single mother and her child in an act of generosity and goodness that deserved an acknowledgement of his male primacy that was for the most part withheld.

With Deva, Manuel advanced from amusing mock-suitor to a man with aspiration to full fatherhood, including paternal instruction and sanctions for failures to obey. He tried to promote himself to patriarch, but Veronica declined to notice. She did not directly resist, she just circumvented him, expressing the opinion that Deva needed very little guidance and that she was doing very well just as things were. Manuel gave Deva orders, which she referred to her mother, who would say that it was up to Deva, and then withstood Manuel's later fury at her daughter's disobedience. When he finally slapped Veronica—he never did hit Deva, sensing that this would be in her mother's eyes the one unforgivable act—she withstood that too, not cowering or reacting, only radiating a pity for the man who had hit her, and who had therefore forfeited his own happiness. The consequence was that Manuel was on occasion reduced to tears at this refusal of his dependent family to let him be a man, and to be fully loved.

There was, however, lovemaking, which the curtain between their bed and Deva's mattress was too flimsy to deny, and from what she could now recall—and these were memories she had long ignored—the noises her mother made were horribly similar to the noises Deva heard coming from herself, the rhythmic gasping, the throaty gargle of an orgasm being wrested from the body as if by a thief, the flailing and the hitting at this perfect loss of dignity. That's how her quiet mother was in lovemaking, unexpectedly furious, and Deva imagined that it was for this transcendent intensity that Manuel continued to put up with the light disregard with which she held his masculine authority. Deva covered her ears, confused by becoming excited from being so close to something so repellent.

And then her mother was ill. She lost weight and spent more time in bed. Her lovely, serene smile remained unchanged in a diminished face. Deva could remember her smile, but not her eyes. Why was that? She was offered no particular explanation for her mother being unwell. Medicines appeared on the bedside table, and in time Manuel retreated from the sick bed and took to sleeping on a roll of foam on the floor next to Deva. While her mother lay quiet, he lay next to Deva, sadly, and told her twelve-year-old self that he did not know what to do, that his money was not enough for the doctors Veronica needed. In any case, she refused to see the doctors, not believing there was anything to be done, just as there had been nothing to be done when her own mother had died young, though not quite as young as this. Manual complained that she would not even talk to him about it, that she had never really been one for talking, and that in truth she had never really let him know her, that she had never really let him in, which he attributed to some lingering love for another man, most probably Deva's father, the Norte Americano who had abandoned her, and whose burden he, Manuel, had taken up, with little appreciation in return. And now she would not even let him help her. "Remember," he said to Deva, "how in the beginning it was you and me who were friends, although you were just a little girl then. We were friends even before I was friends with your mother." He said that perhaps it had been Deva he had fallen for, though when she was ten, he would not have been able to see it, not in the same way he could see it now, her so womanly and able at twelve.

There was that sort of talk. That was Deva's recollection. Memories like that came to her now. And there were nights when in his distress Manuel fell asleep in the gap between her mattress and his, his body close to her, his tears drying while

Deva's were inexplicably held back. She did not have the nerve to push away and wake the exhausted man who must next morning power the city's electricity.

Her mother, always light with her touch on the world, withdrew further. She kissed Deva goodnight, and assured her that she was well and would be all right, and there was no need to worry. She was thinner and sometimes fell into sleep in the middle of a sentence, the effect, Deva now believed, of doses of morphine taken to counteract the pain of a cancer that had migrated through her. She had not known it then—this knowledge came from the heroin addiction in her future that was only just then being sown in her. It seemed to thirteen-year-old Deva, that while her mother was failing to fight for her life, it was only she and Manuel who worried. At night she let Manual come closer in his sleep for comfort, while she lay awake on her back, feeling the intermittent hardness of an erection against her thigh. She did not disturb the hand that sleepily came to rest over her newly mounded breast, with its nipple's unwilled puckering, a nighttime diversion for her thoughts.

At school, Deva let a boy at school put his hand up her skirt and into her underwear, where he fumbled until she assisted his finger into her. He paraded the finger later, holding it under his nose to sniff, so that other boys did the same whenever they saw her, mortifying Deva. In spite of this, Deva later persuaded another boy, famous for his advanced development, and ability to produce semen, to take out his penis and teach her how to pull at it until it came almost immediately into a little puddle in the palm of her hand, astonishing and fascinating and disgusting her. In spite of which, she then went back to the first boy, who had so humiliated her, and offered to perform the same trick on him, perhaps believing that producing smelly stuff from him would counter her own smelly reputation, which did not work and not only because he produced next to nothing. Instead, all Deva achieved was a premature reputation as a puta, which she discovered was less of a burden when embraced. By quick alchemy, she transformed this reputation into one for sophistication, a girl possessing knowledge that other girls craved and few had yet dared to gain.

So, when Manuel finally, tearfully put his hands inside Deva's nightwear, begging her, apologizing, crying, and pleading helplessness, she was not unprepared, and was relieved, at least, by his more skillful touch. Moreover, to his surprise, Manuel found Deva knew how to extract his penis from his underwear, and could bring him to completion with no word exchanged, at which point Manuel whispered, "I love you, Deva," her mother barely six feet away.

Deva was thirteen and Manuel was in his late thirties, so that it was in the course of things, given that Deva had by now taken over all of her mother's roles as woman of the house, that Manuel would plead for Deva to allow him to just place it close, just put it in a little bit, the tip, taking all proper care, and then found he could not help but put it in a whole lot, all the while saying he could not help himself because she was so sweet, and that it was unfair and perverse of God to create such sweetness and center it between the legs of a girl so young, moreover one who he loved. By which time Manual was truly fucking her.

When, the next morning, he discovered that Deva still made his coffee, Manual took to fucking her regularly, Veronica lying quietly behind the curtain, dying. Deva had only much later come to believe that her mother was probably dying more quickly, now she was listening to the poorly concealed betrayal by her daughter, who had replaced her so completely. Deva was thirteen; she might have imagined then that her mother did not notice.

Here, Deva stopped in her account to Harry, and before starting again, told him that she had never before told this to anyone. She had never before even properly allowed these thoughts to form. Then she told him that, if she was now scouringly honest, she must admit that a disgusting part of her had, at the time, exulted in this claim to womanly agency, winning love away from her mother, even though she admired and loved her mother so much, or because of this. It might have been that she thought her mother had betrayed her by refusing to fight for her life—Deva could find no other excuse—by dying so easily and peacefully, abandoning her. For what? The peace of heaven? In any case, not long after Deva became Manuel's lover, her mother moved more swiftly towards death, the cancer that had started out in her breast expanding beyond all capture, and to the end she never uttered a reproach, never failed to whisper that she loved Deva, never lost her gentle smile, until she was finally gone at twenty-nine.

Deva stayed with Manuel for almost another half year. Neighbors who Veronica had never much noticed were by then taking an interest, sensing something unsavory on their doorsteps. And Deva had not proved to be, now the fantasy of competition was gone, competent as either lover or wife. Manuel, at the same time, was a devil of grief and guilt, forever finding fault with her, and berating himself for taking on the burden of someone else's child, a wickedly seductive child, moreover, with the devil in her. His tragedy, he claimed, was to have loved too much.

Relatives Deva barely knew—ones who had stayed distant from Veronica in her shame of single motherhood—now came to rescue Deva, and move her to a nicer home, a better school. Before she had a Norte-Americano's bastard child, before she was orphaned by her own mother's early death, Veronica had been part of a respectable, modestly prosperous, extended family. Deva's grandfather had been an educated man, a botanist, much loved by his only daughter, but who had died tragically before Deva was born. Nevertheless, he passed down intact a belief in the independence and education of women that was thwarted in his daughter, but became fully expressed in Deva. She had never questioned the rightness of it.

"That was my abuse," she said to Harry, when her story was done. "As I remember it. That's how I killed my mother."

Deva had been young enough to believe that she had been in charge. Her forebears, she said now—all the women—were plucked flowers: the mother pregnant at sixteen, the daughter a wife of sorts at thirteen. The abandonment of Veronica by the Norte Americano, she reasoned, had first induced the abusing stepfather, then through Deva's consequent addiction, her own daughter's fatherlessness, damage cascading down the generations. She said that the women of her line were like daffodils in a way, in that their looks attracted. But they were unlike daffodils in that they lacked a poison to deter the predators.

She was sitting close to Harry now, his arm resting around her shoulders. Safe. He murmured, "But most flowers thrive without poison, don't they?"

Deva thought about this and let it go. "Probably," she said, "you should take none of what I say at face value." She straightened herself. Her memories, she now asserted, could be unreliable since they were the sort of memories that people were prone to invent when they needed a specific cause to excuse a more general condition. There had been many cases of such false memories, she assured Harry. But it was also true—she was being analytical now—that these were also the sort of memories people were most likely to suppress because the consequences were unbearably large. So, Harry should be aware of all that, that her memory might be playing tricks, even though it seemed to her not to be the case. "I think," she said, her voice softening, "that I did push my mother towards her death. We were too close. I had been denied a father." She said that she thought now—now that she had allowed these memories to be spoken—that it might not be a taste for promiscuity that was her nature, but a fear of ever again giving power over herself to any one man.

Harry said, "Perhaps now you have remembered once you will not need to keep remembering. Not if you can never know for sure what's true."

They sat silently together for a minute, the subject settling in each of them. Harry broke the silence. "Deva, if my memories return, how will I know whether or not they are true? Would I learn anything at all from remembering?"

Deva pulled herself away from her own past to look at him.

She was horrified that she had not given a thought to what this conversation might mean to Harry. He continued carefully. "Sometimes I think I have something like memories. Nothing much. Just fleeting impressions—scenes that refuse to stay in my mind long enough to be interrogated. They hardly deserve to be called memories. They don't seem to be connected to anything. It's like they were left outside the gates when my brain closed down, and have been wandering around lost ever since."

Deva said nothing, resting gently against the fragility of the moment.

At last, Harry continued. "In these scenes I am always looking down on something from above." He paused. "I don't think I want to say anything to Dr Elliot."

"No," agreed Deva. "Let's not say anything."

In the afternoon, John made his way from his bedroom to the living room along a corridor bright with natural light, a journey repeated sufficiently often that it now seemed like a life. At this time of day, he puttered, while Harry rested in his room. Nadia would be at school and Deva was usually out meeting her friends at University College, or rehearsing at the Miranda, or working at the British Library. John found he had a diminishing inclination to join the world six floors below. The lifelong habit of a daily newspaper had fallen away, and he did not miss it. For the first time in his adult life he knew little of what was going on in the world. As he entered the main room, he felt a quick disappointment to discover that he was not alone. It was the weekend; he had lost track. The day was sunny and the glass doors to the patio were wide open. Outside stood Deva and Nadia, their backs to him, arms around each other's waists. Deva's hair was piled up, approximately held in place by chopstick spears, while Nadia's shorter hair was, by means of clip, turned into a fountain on top of her head. Both wore earrings that glinted in the light. John no longer thought to disapprove.

Mother and daughter were swaying slightly, keeping time, looking out across the roofs of the sunlit city. John moved closer and heard that they were singing, singing softly in Portuguese. It was the first time he had heard Deva sing and now he learned that although her speaking voice was low her singing could range effortlessly high, as it did now, entwining itself around Nadia's sweet, word-conscious delivery. They moved as one, creating their own music and rhythm, loving each other, believing themselves to be alone, complete and unobserved, the beauty incidental to the pleasure. Recollections of his daughters brushed John's mind, his loss of them and all this, how he had got everything wrong, had got his loyalties all wrong. There was the picture again of his two girls, six and eight, looking at him in terror, as their mother crawled towards the door.

These days, tears ambushed him at every turn. Perhaps it was the mini-stroke. In any case he was no longer in full command of himself, far from it. The lilt, the sway, the joining love of mother and daughter, continued, and he took a quiet step backwards so as not to interrupt its play, at which point, Deva, still singing, still moving, turned towards him and smiled, not in the least self-conscious at discovery, and lifted her hand from Nadia's waist to beckon him, so that Nadia, feeling the lifted weight turned too, and held out her thin bare arm in an offer of embrace. He moved past the glass doors towards them, whispering, "Sorry, I was just leaving," and, "Sorry, I can't sing," to which neither replied nor broke off their song, but fixed their attention on his reddened eyes, as if the lyrics he could not understand were about him and carried the exact meaning they wanted to offer him at this moment. He moved closer and Nadia's arm alighted on his waist, her hand finding a fist of shirt to hold, her little hip bumping against his thigh with the rhythm, so that he tried to pick it up, and nearly did, winning a look from Nadia of encouraging approval, causing him to apologize again for his lack of voice, and for Nadia to break her singing long enough to say, "It's all right, John. You can just move with us," tightening the grip of her little painted fingers. He wished this would never end so that finally its motion might wash away forty years of wrongs with its simple right.

Harry also did not remember that, on the same evening he had been embarrassed to be seen driving a Porsche in High Street Kensington, he had found, on a side road, his answered prayer, a parking space large enough not to tax his skills. Even so, the front wheel of the car lodged itself against the curb so that it was stuck askew. Looking up from the job in hand, he discovered the closed faces of a young couple, squeezing past in their more ordinary Volkswagen, apparently judging his maneuver, or coveting his space. There were reasons why he might be watched, he knew, but he did not know enough of such things to judge whether these reasons carried sufficient weight to result in actual watching. Given this ignorance, he elected not to let himself be further troubled by the possibility.

The Miranda was a hundred yards back and as he walked toward it, he girded himself with the consciousness of superior knowledge. He knew about Deva, but she did not know about him. He knew important things about Deva that she did not even know about herself. Later he would decide what to do about her, after he had watched her perform, and perhaps listened to what she had to say. He girded himself thus because he feared the erosion of his resolve.

In all his years in London, Harry had never heard of the Miranda. His brother—the oldest, not the Taliban one, of course—would probably have known of it, and might once have rung this same bell and heard the responding buzz of the opening door in exactly this way. The heavy wood door, with its iron studs, signaled somewhere not English. More Spanish, he thought—that is, Islamic—though he supposed Portugal was the more likely influence for a Brazilian nightclub.

On the few occasions when he had been bullied into going

out on the town to witness his brother's polish and extravagant popularity in the milieu of nightclubs and beautiful women, he had not enjoyed himself and always drank too much. Usually, he had left first, though still late enough to need to pay for a taxi back to Tufnell Park. Now, as he hesitated outside the Miranda, he thought that even at this late evening hour, a housemate in Tufnell Park might be at the kitchen table, able to restore sanity and normality with humor, or sense. Or failing that, his own room might still be left untouched, cozily separated from gaudy London life by its books. He wondered, in retrospect, whether his brother's invitations to share the pleasures of London night life could have been more kind than he had at the time allowed.

He had never asked his brother, who was almost twenty years older, whether he genuinely enjoyed the life in London that had come to be his fate, just as it had been the fate of the middle brother to stay in Pakistan. His sister, Samina, had also accepted her fate, marrying and living in Islamabad, her Oxford degree in English literature, and her appetite for misbehavior, gone to waste. In a way, he was the only one of the four of them who had chosen his own life and escaped. This was an incidental benefit of being the youngest. Wearing his brother's clothes, driving his car, visiting a nightclub, Harry now imagined how it might have been for his brother to have the weight of the family business pressed down upon his shoulders.

A black-and-white photo of Deva was in a glass-covered display case outside the door, together with a menu of just five or six items, ornately handwritten. No prices. He had not noticed the photo earlier—perhaps it had not yet been posted at the time of his reconnoiter. He held the door ajar for a moment to take it in: an enticing, smiling face, amused eyes, a mass of artfully disheveled hair. Attractive, certainly. "Deva from Brazil," it said, and advertised her range, which extended from the rhythms of Rio to the fado of Portugal. Harry doubted that he could distinguish any sort of Latin music. This thought was barely formed when the sound of a band in loud exuberant play poured over him, a crude assault of joy. He grimaced. Over cries of approval from the audience, a woman's voice swooped pure and clear. At the other end of the vestibule, the man who had released the sound held open a thickly padded door and was smiling at the new arrival.

Harry had groomed himself carefully, a fresh haircut, a shave, the light gray Italian suit—it fit well enough, his brother just a little shorter and a little stouter—and thus was more formally attired than the Miranda's manager, a slight, quick man with a tailored shirt worn outside his trousers. In an awkward imitation of his brother's ways, Harry palmed twenty pounds into the manager's hand under cover of a handshake. While the table plans were studied, he looked towards the singer. It was Deva.

The manager started speaking in Portuguese, then made a quick adjustment. No, it was not a problem that he was not a member, Harry was now informed in English, though there would be an extra charge. He followed the manager's look as it scanned the room: a stage with space to dance in front of it, sinuous waitresses moving between close-pressed tables, shadowed booths around the walls. It was compact and crowded. "Somewhere quiet," he said into the manager's ear.

"Quiet?"

"I mean not too close to the band. Is it possible?"

The manager nodded possibility. "You're expecting guests?"

"Just myself for now."

"And dinner?"

"Yes," he replied, though he was not hungry. He knew his drinks bill would be a disappointment.

From the shadow of the booth, one hand curled around a glass of Perrier, he settled to consider Deva, wondering how he would play things, and whether he would be able to talk to her, even though much about her was already decided. At ease on the stage, gorgeous and adored, she seemed intimidatingly immune to any disadvantage. In any case there was nothing to be done for now, but to listen to the music and trifle with his food.

Looking back, taking the long view, his brother's fate had been set the day the Soviets invaded Afghanistan. It was, by coincidence, the same year Harry was born, delivered prematurely in a Peshawar hospital after his mother's perilous jeep journey down from the mountains. Of course, the Afghanis had to resist the invasion. Of course, the unifying power of Islam was intrinsic to the mujahedin resistance. And, of course, America saw a Cold War opportunity there, to fight its enemy by utilizing the lives of others. And once that decision was made, it was inevitable that the US and Pakistan looked for allies among the tribal leaders in the border areas, to channel the money and the arms. Men like Harry's father, an Afridi malik from a clan with land in both countries. Of course, his father would have been irresistible to them, a rare English speaker with a city home in Peshawar and roots in the FATA mountains, and village homes on both sides of the border. In Peshawar his father owned a small fleet of Bedford lorries. Perfect. Inevitable.

Nor did his father have any choice, really, given his responsibilities to his people, but to accept this offer of support for the mujahedin. He could only manage the consequences as best he could. And, when the US further perceived that their anti-narcotic policies were not only ineffective in curbing local opium poppy production and the heroin trade, but were also hated by their new allies, the arrival of the next good idea was equally inevitable: the US would instead facilitate the opium and heroin trades, so that the tribal areas might finance the mujahedin themselves. The cost of the war would ultimately be borne by heroin addicts on the streets of Europe and America, not the American taxpayer. Brilliant! The strategy was also popular among the tribesmen, who both prospered economically, and were confirmed in their conviction of their spiritual superiority to the West. Managing the opium and heroin trade, while keeping the drugs away from his own people, was the first task assigned to Harry's oldest brother. Delivering the money and arms to the mujahedin fell to the middle brother, who in this company—inevitably, of course—discovered a deeper faith and a cause to join.

The family became very rich. Not to have become rich would have been suspicious. Wanting to be rich was an aspiration the Americans trusted. In effect, Harry's father was turned into something that he had never sought to be and which did not suit him: a drug lord. After the Soviets left Afghanistan in 1989, he quickly shut down the drug trade and turned the family money into legitimate businesses. They bought the Baker Street house and sometimes they stayed there as a family. Later, his oldest brother moved to London to manage things. Harry and his sister, Samira, were kept in England, out of harm's way, to complete their education, he to boarding school and she to university. Back in Pakistan, his middle brother remained devout and militant, so that when Afghanistan was once again invaded, this time by the Americans, he was already part of the resistance of the faithful, this time calling itself the Taliban. All this, Harry saw, had been inevitable.

But Harry had kept out of things, the handsome, gentle poet in London with nice, serial girlfriends, who were always educated, and usually English. He turned his back on the other options offered: wealth, fundamentalism, marriage. He thought of them as his siblings' tragedies. His own life, he thought, had not been inevitable. He had consciously resisted the roles offering by unspooling geopolitics. His mild choice was, in its way, the most radical and hubristic of them all. Harry, the self-invented English poet. But he wondered how a poet was supposed to engage with a word like "squirters"? It was what American drone operators in their remote locations called the injured or dying Pakistani civilians collaterally wounded by a drone strike. "Squirters." What could a Martian Romantic do with that?

The rousing music ended and Deva turned from the microphone to speak to the band, which reformed itself so that one of them moved his chair forward into the light, settling an acoustic guitar on his lap, while the others leaned back, wiping brows and putting down their instruments, bending forward to pick up their drinks. The couples on the dance floor thinned, then dispersed entirely, understanding something. Deva looked up to smile at her audience, a broad smile transmitting unreserved goodwill. Even when all she did was to move aside the microphone and talk quietly to the guitarist, the audience's eyes stayed on her. Her dress was long and midnight blue. The neckline was a tease. Thirties or thereabouts—about his own age—and at ease with her body. Harry flashed on a picture from childhood of women, fully robed, bathing in a secluded stream, the cotton cloth clinging to them. Deva's presence managed to be both sexy and maternal, giving Harry the sense that she might cheerfully say yes to a man, but that if she said no, her refusal would be kind. Was this in her favor? Recently, Harry had not thought much about sex.

With the rearrangements complete and the barrier of a microphone removed, Deva took a lacy black scarf and covered her shoulders, abruptly and strikingly modest. Her posture and expression stiffened. She waited for silence. When it was complete, the guitarist bent over in pained concentration to extract notes of a spare clarity, which gathered into a sighing music that Harry felt he almost knew. Deva stood motionless, waiting for her moment. Then, she tilted back her head and closed her eyes, her voice ringing out above the guitar, naked and strong. Its mournful beauty sent a shiver through Harry. The guitar's sweet complaint chased Deva to greater heights, while she remained bravely still, drawing great breaths between the song's declarations, which could only be of suffering. A passionate sadness had routed the room's dancing and laughter, and released the audience into a deeper life, the full embrace of tragedy. Deva's voice grew more hoarse, straining for volume and intensity. She stamped her foot just once, as if frustrated that there was no more of herself to give.

Harry leaned forward, intent on establishing that it was tears not perspiration that ran down her cheeks. She did not brush them aside. Sadness was not to be brushed aside. He understood nothing of the Portuguese, but he knew he was hearing poetry. She was singing for him. Deva was pleading for the freedom of the anguish imprisoned inside, offering an ocean of suffering into which to throw himself. If she could sing like this, she must have known heartbreak. They were orphans, both of them. In his booth, wrapped in the shadow and in Deva's voice, he heard himself quietly keening.

It was already a month, and he had not yet stopped to mourn. Though he supposed he would inherit, he had not thought about his father's money. It had not even occurred to him to buy a suit for tonight, or even shoes that fit. His brother's shoes, he noticed, were very soft, and so were comfortable enough. He had never thought about wealth as meaning something as simple as soft shoes. Wealth, he had thought of mainly as what separated people from experience and truth.

Deva ended the song abruptly, decreeing silence. He held his breath. For long moments there was no reaction, then Deva bowed, her hand going to her neckline to keep it modest, and when she came up smiling, the black scarf falling from her, the monkeys of applause were released. He did not join them, unable to leave just yet the company of grief.

It was later that same night, when Deva came into her bedroom, wearing nothing but a towel wrapped around her hair, that Harry was stuck by the thought that they came from the world's opposing poles of modesty. When he had done as instructed and moved Deva's clothes from her bed to a chair, a circumlocution of the family servants in Peshawar jumped back at him from childhood: "female undergarments." How was it, when he had started the evening in possession of a full authority over Deva's life, he had come to tidying her underwear? Deva moved around him, easy in her nakedness, the seductiveness he had seen at the club discarded with her clothes. Her breasts had lost their tease, but were more lovely. "Come on, Harry," she had said, plucking at his shirt. "Take that off."

After they had made love, while he waited for Deva to return to bed from the bathroom, he was shamed by the conviction of his treachery. He had thought to harm Deva, but had taken comfort from her. It had been wrong, this joining, but also relief from his utter solitude.

When Deva returned, hurrying back to the bed, she curled quickly into sleep, but Harry had not found rest. He could not imagine the morning with Deva and wanted to leave before she woke. In the composure of her face, he saw dreams passing under her eyelids, her face glowing softly with the indirect light of streetlamps. He had the impulse to leave something of himself, to offer Deva something significant, and took from his pocket the photo of John he carried with him to steady his intention. He dropped it on the low table where Deva had thrown her things the night before. Nothing, yet something.

It was nearly bedtime. Deva and John were sitting on the couch, extending the day.

Deva said, "The women in your café—the one in your town?"

"Omar's Bookstore Cafe"

"Yes, Omar's. You know they talked about you?"

"Not really. They had a lot to say about everything."

"They had theories about you. You were a mystery. At least one thought you were attractive."

"Which one?"

"I think it was the Indian. They also thought you were lonely. And unfriendly."

"That's fair."

"They couldn't imagine what you did."

"You know, I used to listen to those women sometimes. You couldn't help it. The table of international women, I called it. And I thought it would be wonderful to sit with such a warm, intelligent group of women."

"Yet apparently you didn't even say hello."

"Not really. I wouldn't know what to say to them."

"They were very easy to talk to."

"For you. I didn't have any words then. Even fewer than I do now."

"But were you lonely, like they said?"

"Well, now I might call it lonely. But then it felt like something else. I suppose it just felt like everything had ended, and there was nothing to hope for. My main ambition was to get through the day. It was all about disciplined habit. I went to the gym every morning and talked with other retired men there. Then I went to Omar's and, if it was a good day, the girl behind the counter would smile at me. That would be pretty much it. I marked the days off with mealtimes. I read the *New York Times*, and kept briefed on foreign affairs. I maintained the house and yard."

"Your family?"

"Oh, I lost them a long time ago."

"Dead?"

"No. No, I acted badly towards them. I'd had a difficult trip abroad and something my wife did made me lose my temper. It's something I'm ashamed of. I told Harry all about it the other day. He's the only person I've ever told. Strange to think of that—that it should be him. Anyway, it was the final straw for my wife. We'd already gone our separate ways. When I retired, I could have gone to live among some ex-colleagues in Maine, messing about in boats and so on, but I didn't want to see them again. So, I chose to be alone in New Hampshire. Just the gym and Omar's for society. Ticking over until the clock stopped."

"That's crazy. What happened to you?"

"I messed things up. Messed up my life and some others. As a matter of fact, I'd been thinking about summing it all up in a memoir of sorts at about the time you turned up. Drawing a line under my life. One of the women at the café worked for a local outfit that helps people write their memoirs. You Must Remember This, it's called. Her card was tucked into the café notice board. She may even own the business. Anyway, their idea is to interview old people about their lives, write it up for them, and make it into a book for their families. For a steep price. It seemed a lazy way to write a memoir. But I worried that when the woman came to interview me she might be so disgusted that she would refuse to write it. And then I wouldn't be able to go to Omar's anymore."

"So, what happened?"

"I didn't do it."

"Because you were scared?"

"Yes. But also someone asked me not to. Then you turned up."

"Your family told you not to?"

"No, my old employer."

"Secrets?"

"Yes. But I haven't given up the idea. What can anyone do to me?"

"So, you'll do it when you return?"

John thought, then said, "I'm not sure. Maybe I'm telling everything to you and Harry instead."

"Even the disgusting bits?"

"Seems so."

"The overseas trip that upset you and broke up your marriage? Was that Pakistan?"

John considered his reply, then said, "No, that was Latin America. A very long time ago. The Cold War years, you know. Pakistan came a bit later. Still the Cold War. Pakistan wasn't so bad."

"Latin America was worse than Pakistan?"

"Yes. In Latin America we were supporting military dictators. In Pakistan we were fighting against a Soviet invasion of Afghanistan. The difference was that in Pakistan we were mainly on the same side as the people. I never got that feeling in South America."

Deva said, "No, in South America, the US was always on the side of the generals."

"I'm afraid so. But when I first went to Pakistan, I felt good about my job. I was concerned with civilian matters, especially drug substitution programs. You know, persuading farmers to stop growing opium and feeding the heroin trade."

"And how did that go?"

"Oh, that didn't work at all."

John explained that no crop was better suited to the soil and climate, than opium poppies, or as valuable, or as easy to transport. The farmers didn't want to give it up. But it did give John the pretext to get to know the leaders in the tribal areas on the border with Afghanistan. By chance, he was on a trip to the northwest tribal areas when there was an earthquake, in which several remote mountain hamlets were buried by mudslides. A tribal malik came to him and asked for help. There was little government presence in the Federally Administered Tribal Areas and no aid had been offered. In Peshawar and Islamabad, the provincial and national governments did not even seem to know that there had been a disaster. John toured the area with the malik, traveling the last part on horseback, and saw for himself: dozens dead, hundreds homeless, the roads and irrigation channels all destroyed, with the winter snows just starting.

John had accepted the disaster as a gift. After the shock of Brazil and the sordid horror of Tania, he was desperate to keep alive an idea of himself as someone who could do good. He threw himself tirelessly into helping turn over the rubble of mud-brick houses, then made the perilous journey down to Islamabad to argue for a helicopter and relief supplies. He returned to supervise the unloading and distribution, risking his life to do so. The tribal leader who had first approached him, the only one in the region who spoke English, took John to heart and opened up Pushto hospitality to him. Although Westerners were generally despised, he was made the exception, and was feted. When the Pushto made you their friend, John explained to Deva, you were an absolute friend until death. They would literally give their lives for you.

It was the time when American support for the mujahedin fighting the Soviets was increasing. The policy was administered by Pakistani intelligence so that the Americans could keep their hands clean, but John now found himself in a crucial position. He was the only American attached to the Islamabad embassy with a tribal leader for a friend. He could visit the border area, and see for himself how the American arms and money were, or were not, reaching the mujahedin. Instead of reducing the flow of drugs, he ended up supporting the poppy farmers and facilitating the opium and heroin trade that was supporting the war effort. He stayed in Pakistan until 1989, when the Soviets were defeated and left Afghanistan.

John said to Deva, "War is never good, but in this case I felt I had been doing something not bad."

"And then?"

"Well, then my superiors thought my personal connection to the malik was too strong and they moved me to another country, and eventually back to Washington. I didn't return to Pakistan for over twenty years—until last year, in fact. Different times now, of course. Now, America is the invading enemy. But friendship and hospitality are an absolute among the Puhk-toon—along with honor, revenge, and never, never forgetting. I wanted to go and visit my old friend one last time—he's even older than me—and my previous employers didn't object. They even facilitated it. They are currently invested in the idea that the border tribes secretly do not like the Taliban, but are afraid to say so. I thought that was nonsense but said I would keep my ears open. I told my old friend the truth about my visit. I wasn't spying. And it was good to see him. He was still a friend. My best remaining friend, probably. That was my last overseas trip. There hadn't been anything for five years before that. Ironic, wasn't it, that my closest remaining friend lived in the tribal areas of Pakistan. I think I wanted to be reminded of something I could be proud of."

"But in the past you were a sort of spy. A bit of a spy."

John made a face. "Well, yes, intelligence. But mostly above board. It's just that we Americans are insanely in love with secrecy. Even when it serves no purpose."

"So, what was it that you thought would disgust the women from Omar's?"

"Oh, I imagined that representing the American foreign policy at all would be enough—they're all academics and liber-als. Most of them are foreigners. But I was thinking of things that were more personal. Well, a mixture, I suppose. The politi-cal is personal. Is that the saying? No, it's the other way around, isn't it? The personal is political. But my version seemed more true in my case."

"Are we back in Latin America?"

"I suppose we are."

"But not Brazil? You said you hadn't worked in Brazil."

John took a breath. "I'm sorry, Deva. I did lie to you. Professional habit. I didn't really know you then. I'm sorry. In fact, Brazil was the first place I worked. I won't lie to you anymore. And I don't seem able to lie to Harry at all."

"Yes, why is it impossible to lie to Harry? I end up telling him everything too. What do you think that is?"

John hesitated, then said, "Maybe it's because he's unable to lie to us. I mean, how could he? Without memories? I think that the lying part of his brain just isn't there. He's infected us with truth telling. And he knows when other people are lying. Have you noticed that? Then, he just looks puzzled. Almost pitying. Like he's sympathizing with your inexplicable mistake. He never says anything. It makes it worse."

"I know. He's never shocked. Never judges. I love him." Deva stopped, having surprised herself.

John said, "Yes, I can see that. In a way, I do too. Not the same way, perhaps."

"Who knows? Anyway, there's nothing sexual between us. The first time I met him we had sex right away. It was okay. Complicated, but okay. Now it doesn't matter how close I sit, there's nothing like that. I've never told him about the first time—that we were lovers. He doesn't seem to know and my instinct is that he would find it disturbing. Don't say anything, please."

"I won't. But you said he's never disturbed."

"Okay, so maybe this is for me. I like things the way they are. Anyway, John, what is it about your unspeakably disgusting life that would frighten the memoir women from Omar's? You sort of changed the subject. Are we still talking about Brazil?"

"Well, probably, we are. Partly. You know, Deva, I can't exactly explain why, but if I'm going to talk about this, I want Harry here. Maybe if Harry was here, I'd feel easier."

"That bad?"

"Maybe. Confusing, at least. You know, you mean something to me, Deva. You and Nadia. I don't want to lose you. And I don't want to have secrets from you."

"What about Harry?"

"Well, Harry said that nothing I could say would ever make him dislike me. It was a strange thing to say. Out of the blue. But I believe him."

J ohn! What's this nonsense about no phones?" Gwen was shouting into hers. "We've seen neither hide nor hair of you."

"I had to give mine up. House rules."

"What nonsense!"

Dr Elliot had told John that his employer needed to talk to him. John asked whether he meant Harry, and Dr Elliot said, "Don't be ridiculous."

"Hello, Gwen. How are you?" he said now, to slow her down.

"Never mind all that. I don't like phones. I can hardly hear. Is he your friend's son, this Harry? Our terrorist."

"Possibly. It fits. Time, place, the London house. I can't be sure."

"What have you told the Brits?"

"The same."

"They say you're having a vacation."

"I'm winning trust."

"Not enjoying yourself, then?"

"Well, you said I should."

"You like the girl? The Brazilian."

"I do. Not in that way."

"Does Harry know about his family? And your part?"

"No. What part is that?"

"You know what part. It's time to pay the piper, John. Find out what he knows and what's planned. It's not like it isn't urgent."

"He's fragile."

"And we care? He's a terrorist. Break him."

"That isn't my role."

"Well, it turns out the Brits aren't any good at it. So, it's on you. And whatever you find out, is ours. I'm so tired of this."

"Of what? The business?"

"Of babying you. All your self-indulgent regrets and scruples. Your loose cannon agonizing. A memoir! What was that outfit called—You Must Remember This? Lord save us! No. No, John, you must not remember this. Why do you think they have me still supervising you? I'm eighty. And I'm too old for patience. Lives at stake, John. Lives at stake. Lives on our side. So, get on with it. That's the message. Get on with it."

"Or what?"

"Why go there? Get it done and come home to fester in your rustic misery. Your country will be grateful. Etcetera."

John explained to Harry and Deva that it was the event in his life that was most secret, and that had most haunted him. It was, he said, one of the three horrors that had rushed at him at the time of the photo. He had already confided one of them, the time he hit his wife. This one might be even worse. It felt even worse.

"And the third?" asked Deva.

John said, quietly, "It's more recent. I'm not ready for that yet." He looked at Harry, who nodded, as if he understood.

"It was my first independent field assignment. I wasn't much over thirty. To Brazil. It ended with a girl I cared about telling me I'd raped her, and spitting in my face." He briefly lifted his eyes to Deva. He saw her features hardening.

Then John told his story of the awfulness of Concordia, the unsavory murderers supported by his government and the generals, the girl, Veronica, who had lost her father, and how she had saved his sanity, until, at the very end, the understanding between them had contorted itself into the moment of horror when Veronica said, "Jim, you rape me."

For John, the memory ended there, with the shock of it. He had long ago forgotten that they were calm together afterwards, subsiding into quiet, and even tenderness. They had been gentle in their disentangling, John fussing at the sight of blood, and Veronica making light of this mess and any hurt of her. He had advised her to wash herself.

On her return to him, she told John that she should not have spat at him—it was so unlike her. This, he barely heard, his shocked attention fixed on her earlier accusation and on the blood on the sheet, this further evidence that his local advisors were liars. He was thinking that Veronica's first should have been a boy, sweet and awkward and skinny. He told her this and

Veronica was arch in her response, at his ever supposing she was not a virgin, and at his supposing that he knew what was best for her. She smiled to show that she was teasing. Sometime later, after long silences, while Veronica busied herself restoring order to the room, in a moment John had never recalled, she mused that she was happy, actually, that he had been her first. She said that she had considered regret but had decided against it. Surely, it was better that her first was an experienced man, and one she knew, and who she already liked. And she had been part of it, hadn't he noticed? She had chosen him. She had kissed him. If John heard this at all, his mind, already steeped in all manner of guilt and falsehood, resisted it, and thirty-three years later he was convinced that no such mitigation could have existed.

The rest, the travel arrangements for Veronica, her packing, the goodbyes, were so ordinary, so redolent of dozens of uncomfortable goodbyes, that the specifics did not stick with him. What fixed to remind him of Veronica—a jewel set so perfectly within the setting of his self-disgust—was Veronica spitting in his face and the words, "Jim, you rape me." As he now told it to Harry and Deva, the story ended there. The girl had told him that he had raped her. She had spat at him. This was, he said, his greatest shame, the kernel of a general shame that had accumulated over the years and dogged his life, and which he had now for the first time revealed to another living person.

When he finished, Deva and Harry were silent. John did not look at them. Then Deva said quietly, "You are Jim."

He looked up at her, tugged from his self-absorption by her tone.

She repeated, "You called yourself Jim. My mother's name was Veronica. You're the Norte Americano who abandoned my mother."

John looked puzzled, scared, saying, "What do you mean?"

"My mother told me my father was a good man helping poor people. And that she even named me for him. Apparently, you are the father who abandoned me. But you weren't a good man, were you? Not at all. And your name wasn't even Jim, was it?" Her face had turned white.

"What?" John, who had been absorbed in his own story, now struggled to step out of it. "What? What do you mean, named for me?"

"I just got it. Your Development of Amazonia project. Your sleazy cover. That was Deva. Right?"

He remembered now. It had been written in capitals on the side of his jeep: DEVA.

"That's why I'm the only Deva in the world. It's not a name anywhere. I did the research. I'm just the acronym for a fake American aid project. Wonderful! I wait a lifetime to meet my father. Then his name is fake. And my name is fake. He's a fake. Wonderful! And I'm the result of his sort of, maybe raping my mother. And the people who killed my grandfather worked for him. I feel like a complete fool. I even liked you! You're the most disgusting man in the world." Deva's eyes blazed. She stood up, shaking, then turned towards her room, and ran off.

John did not move a muscle. He had told his story hoping for Harry's absolution. If he had been almost dead before, he was more dead now. He had found a new daughter, and destroyed her. He loved her. She hated him.

It came to Harry that, of the three of them, he was now the only one capable of useful action. He was unpracticed at being capable, and unused to action. Since his accident, he had not been called upon, but now he saw there was a need. There had been a human disaster. In his home, under his care, there had been a human disaster. Somehow—he could not work out how—he had been the instrument of catastrophe. It was his to correct, a problem only he could address. He knew what to do. He stood and went over to the motionless John. Not even tears had dared to move in John. Harry bent down to him and kissed the older man on the head, and said with quiet certainty, "You are not to blame." Then, "I'll go to Deva." Then, "It will be all right." He took John's hand and led his guest to his room, settled him there, and closed the curtains against the light. "Sleep now," he said, shutting the door carefully. "Sleep will help you."

Next Harry went to find Nadia where she was playing on her own. "Your mamie's napping," he said. "So is John."

"I'm not tired," said Nadia.

"Me neither."

"But you're always napping."

"I know. But not today. Now, I want to know what happened to Serena since I last saw her. Ming wants to know."

Nadia considered this, then announced, "Serena has a new friend."

"Can I meet him?"

"He's a girl." Nadia giggled. "I mean she's a girl. I'm silly."

"Go ahead," said Harry. "Get things ready. I'll be with you in a little while."

"With Ming?"

"Yes, Ming too, of course. And, Nadia, you know that puppy we've been talking about? I think it's time he joined us."

"Mrs. Slater said she didn't want a puppy."

"Well, it will not be Mrs. Slater's puppy."

Harry felt energized with purpose. He found Deva flung across her bed on her stomach, her pillow wet. Closing the door behind him, he sat down next to her. She said, huskily, "If I had some heroin now, I'd take it."

Harry waited.

She turned towards him, her face red. "Harry, do you know why I went to Washington? I went there to find my father. Jim, my father. The man my mother told me about. I used the excuse of my research project to visit all the agencies he might have worked for. The government departments wouldn't tell me anything, just like the consulate in Brazil wouldn't tell my mother anything when she found out she was pregnant. All I found out was that there had been some regional projects operating in the area, but nothing in Concordia itself. I was an intern at the World Bank for my George Washington master's and the Brazilian representative there tried to help me. Helped himself to me too." A tiny hiccough of a laugh from an earlier Deva momentarily broke through. "He also told me there were no development projects in Concordia at that time. He said that this Jim was probably a spy, and I'd never find out about him. And you know, I didn't believe him. I told him he was mistaken, because my mother had told me about my father and the good work he was doing in Concordia. This was the father I've held inside me all these years. The good, kind, handsome Jim. I stopped looking for him, and just settled for the knowledge that my father was a good man, who had passed on to me a share of his intelligence and health—and enough good looks to make me worthy of my mother."

For a moment Deva was silent, turning things over before continuing. "My mother never said a single bad word about Jim. She rarely said anything bad about anyone. And what did I do? I stole her man from right in front of her while she was dying.

I did that. I helped her to die. Maybe that's the part of me I get
from John."

Deva's tears broke out again, and it was time for Harry to
reach down to hold her, and pull her body into his. Gently, his
embrace grew firmer, their bodies closer. Harry felt himself
move into her pain, and her pain into him. Deva's wracked
body relaxed and conformed to his. Her tears were soaking into
his shirt. She had found and lost a father, but was not alone,
was not even separate. She moved her face to Harry's neck so
that he felt the slowing of her breath there. He held steady the
support of his embrace. He was healing her, drawing out the
poison. Harry knew he could do this. They stayed immobile
for long minutes until gradually Deva's sense of her separate
existence returned to her. Her breasts were squashed against
Harry's chest; she was breathing in the smell of him.

They pulled apart and looked at each other. Deva took
Harry's hand and drew it to her heart, then clasped it between
her own hands.

Harry said, "Now, you must sleep. Can you sleep?"
Deva nodded. Suddenly, she was very, very tired.

"I have a date with Nadia," said Harry. "I need to be Ming.
And, oh, I'm sorry, but I promised her the puppy. Never mind
Mrs. Slater."

Deva smiled and murmured, "A puppy. Good," and closed
her eyes.

Both John and Deva were sleeping now. Harry was gratified.
They would be healing in their sleep. They were the unconscious ones while he was more awake than at any time since his
accident. Something new.

When Veronica's family had receded from the shamed girl and her fantastic claim of an absent foreign paternity for her illegitimate child, and from the dangerous taint around her father's death, she declined to be bitter. She found a humble job in a fabric shop, whose owner tolerated Deva and who grew dependent on Veronica's quick arithmetic. She made an art of poverty, by never wanting more. Deva understood early on that her mother would never ask for anything, and that there was around her an aura that let others know that this integrity was impregnable. The self-sufficiency of mother and daughter held a playful, quiet joy within the life of daily difficulty.

At six, Deva left the cocoon of beautiful young mother and enchanting infant daughter to encounter the rougher world of school where her new schoolmates wasted no time informing her that what she was lacking, what others had, or were ashamed not to have, was a father. When Deva asked, Veronica at first replied with the assertion that Deva was hers entirely and that there could be no happier arrangement. Later, this was amended with the confirmation that of course Deva had a father, everyone did, and hers was a particularly wonderful father, who happened to live far away in a different country. Later still, when classroom taunts included the accusation that the reason she knew nothing of her father was because her mother was a puta, Veronica told her daughter that she knew exactly who was her father. He was a Norte Americano, and lived in North America and, for fabulous North American reasons, could not be expected to be there with them. Later still, she conceded his name, Jim, but never a second name. And later still, when she judged that Deva was old enough to comprehend, she said that she had never loved any man but Jim, and that whatever the confusions of paternity among her schoolmates, there should be no such confusion for Deva.

When would her father join them, Deva had then wanted to know. She started at about this time to scan the streets for real or imagined North Americans, and so as to stop this habit from turning into obsession Veronica told Deva that Jim would never come. He would not come because he did not know where they were. He did not in fact know that he had a daughter at all, and if Veronica had wanted to tell him she had no way of doing so since she did not know where he was, except that he was in North America. And in any case, it was better for Deva to be content, as she was herself content, than to indulge in the sort of frenzied longing that she thought she had detected recently in her daughter. And, in any case, a search for her father would not only have no chance of success, but would also entail the sort of expense that they were in no position to imagine. Then there was the matter of upsetting both Jim's life and theirs. And they were happy, weren't they? Veronica had possessed, considering her youth, a calm wisdom that Deva had always admired without being able to fully emulate.

Around the time Deva was nine—a little before she determined to find her mother an alternative man and herself a surrogate father—Veronica told Deva the story of how she met Jim. She said she had been very young. She had found herself at sixteen in a rough town on the edge of the Amazon. It was a tormented, hellish town where men were half human and half alcohol, and were out to grab whatever they could. These were men with all the goodness squeezed out of them by greed and hardship. She had not gone there alone, of course, but with her father, Deva's grandfather, a wonderful man, an educated man, and she, Veronica, had been allowed to accompany him due to her own insistent begging. He was an expert in forest plants and was undertaking important scientific work. Veronica said she particularly wanted to be with him in this rough place because her father was not himself a rough man, and she would therefore be his entire life for as long as they stayed there. Her mother, his wife, had no appetite for such a place, and her health, even then, would not have allowed it, so that at sixteen Veronica could be her clever, funny father's companion, as long as her schoolwork did not suffer. Her father had loved her and had arranged, while he took a short field trip into the forest, for her to stay safe in a secure little house.

She had in fact enjoyed her first two days of independence, avoiding the town's roiling filth, washing and ironing her clothes, spending the evenings making such good progress in her schoolwork that her father was bound to be impressed.

The two days had turned into three with no word from her father. She kept to her strict routine. She told herself that the sound of distant gunfire and the scent of violence that pervaded the town had nothing to do with her, or her father, the fastidious surveyor of natural resources. When the days continued to pass without news, she did not know what to do other than to each day eat less and less of the food they had bought before her father left, and to eke out her little money. Then one day, when she was becoming desperate and feeling completely alone, Deva's father had introduced himself, a cleanly dressed and rather shy man, quite different from the other men of the town. He was a Norte Americano and spoke a charmingly rudimentary Portuguese. In many ways, he was a man like her father, not all that much younger. He was educated and polite, a man also, like her father, doing good work alone and far away from home. He was trying to do something to improve the lives of poor rural people, and she could see he was a little sad in his loneliness. Jim had helped her and protected her. He was her angel. He sent people out to search for her father and had bought food and bottled water. He had protected her from the rougher elements in the town. Otherwise, there was no knowing what might have happened. He had taken an interest in her homework, particularly, she remembered, the botany and English. "Your father," she said to Deva, "was the kindest man, and the result of that kindness is you." In Veronica's story, Deva was conceived by kindness.

At the time, Veronica had needed to come to terms with the horrifying disappearance of her father. She left the matter with their local police, which was like pouring water down a drain, and with Jim's money and protection returned home to her mother in Rio, where they had clung to each other in misery. Soon after, even before she had understood she was pregnant, Jim fell out of contact. Perhaps he had returned to the United States, or moved on to another project. She did not know, and feared something worse. She went with her mother to press the Rio police for further information about her father, but they showed no interest in them, except as women. Nor had Veronica been able to find out anything more about Jim, or his work, which she knew only by the project name on the side of his jeep. When her pregnancy was indisputable, they had gone to the American consulate, only to be told they had insufficient information to even attempt to trace anyone, and that she must have remembered wrongly since they knew of no such project and no such American. They had been nastily unhelpful to the pregnant teenage girl who wanted an American as the father for her child.

Veronica's mother died not long after Deva was born and so they were left alone, the two of them. The daughter was her mother's happiness. As Veronica later described it to Deva, large international forces beyond her comprehension had brought Jim to her side, and large international forces had taken him away again, and what had been left behind by this receding tide had been a perfect pearl of love. Without the blessing of Deva—that is, without the love of Jim—Veronica's loss of her parents would have been unbearable.

This story was never neatly told, but was released to Deva in pieces over time, as a mother bird might feed her young. Deva now understood for the first time that her mother's story of Jim—or John—was suspect, a story favored over other versions that might be less palatable to a child. If not, then why had she spat at him? And her mother had probably never known what Deva now knew: the falseness of Jim's good works.

While Harry watched over her, Deva slept, and in her sleep the stories of her conception became a tangled skein, hate and love impossible to separate.

The day after he told the story of the rape, John did not leave his room, and saw nothing of Deva or Harry. He fell in and out of wakefulness, but did not think to move. Mrs. Slater left him dinner on a tray, which he ignored, and so stumbled into a second night alone. Sometimes he imagined he was in solitary, in a cell, waiting for his trial. Sometimes he wished to be sentenced to death.

What arrived the following day was not a trial, but a puppy. It nosed its way into the room where John lay motionless on his back. He had been trying out the idea of reassembling himself for life, but the idea would not take. There should be a point of view from which his life had been worthwhile, or at least not harmful, or at least constructed of honest mistakes, on which basis he might respect himself enough to carry on. There should be a version of his life that was moved in part by love, or by truth. These thoughts were a starter motor that whirred and whirred without engaging any gears. There was nothing he could put right and, in any case, putting things right would be an undeserved satisfaction.

The puppy, golden-furred with a black nose too big for it, made its way to his bedside with an eager-to-please, head-down, whole-body wag, delighted to have found another warm human in this far reach of the house, eager to ingratiate himself, and not in the least inclined to judge. John looked down at the puppy now it had reached the bed. If he was to live up to his current view of himself, and presumably Harry's and Deva's, shouldn't he want to give this puppy a kick? He didn't. Instead, he reached out his hand and let the puppy lick his palm, then scratched him behind the ears and on his rump, so that the puppy became ecstatic with the pleasure of his company and John gratefully lifted him onto the bed where he walked all over John's body with little pawing massages, seeking and discovering in John an exciting new topography rich with scents.

It was a cheap gratification, wasn't it, the affection of a puppy who knew nothing of human morality, but he found himself wanting to believe that a puppy's innocence intuited good from evil, and that its trust—it had now curled up in John's armpit and dropped into sleep—was a true verdict. John let himself follow the puppy into blameless puppy dreams.

The padding in the corridor outside was Nadia, looking for her new pet. She was calling out its name, "Sunny!" in mock annoyance. This was, John understood with a fresh shock—accepting completely that Deva could not be wrong—his granddaughter. Into the increasing aridity of age, he had been delivered a gorgeous, brilliant daughter, and an enchanting granddaughter, but their being born of violence, the world's and his, meant he could claim no part of them.

There was something in the back of John's mind that was asking for attention. Deva had no idea he was her father before he told his story, just as he had no idea that she was his daughter. She had just been sitting there, listening, while he was transported by his confession, her legs folded under her in a relaxed posture that showed no anticipation of a shock. He had mainly been looking at Harry, drawn into Harry's receptivity. This meant, now he formulated the idea, that either he and his daughter had come to be in this same place at the same time by astonishing coincidence, or that some mechanism intrinsic to their relationship had caused it to happen. It all had something to do with Harry. Harry had given the photograph of him to Deva, and the photograph had brought them all together. Harry had left the photo with Deva before he lost his memory, so he knew what he was doing. But the two of them had only just met. And his own life had never crossed Deva's; he didn't even know he had a daughter. He could not make it make sense.

Nadia now poked her head around John's door, wearing her much-admired sweet smile. Apparently, Nadia had no inkling of the drama. Her current interest was focused on the puppy, not John, and she was determined to make her name for the puppy stick. "Sunny," she was saying. "There you are, Sunny. You are a naughty, naughty Sunny."

Sunny, cozy under John's arm, raised his heavy head with effort in response to this call for yet another round of play. Nadia climbed onto the bed and lay down, nuzzling Sunny with her own puppy nose. For long seconds they were a warm family of dogs snuggled in their den. John held his breath.

Just as Sunny had drawn Nadia to John's room, so Nadia drew Deva. She pushed the door fully open and stood at the threshold, dazed, a cloud of numbing sleep still enclosing her. It was two days since they last saw each other. Deva's hair was a tangle and she was tugging a pink dressing gown around herself. On her feet were ridiculous fluffy pink mules with an artificial blue flower attached to the front of each. Without makeup, her lips were pale. Her eyes were red. He thought, She's come to protect Nadia and take her away from me. Deva was not smiling. Her eyes, somehow darker now, stayed on John, unafraid and untouchable. He recalled Veronica's regarding eyes before she spat at him.

"Nadia," said Deva in a husky voice, "why don't you take Sunny to Mrs. Slater? Ask her to fill his water bowl." Obediently, Nadia slipped off the bed and picked up the puppy with a rough awkwardness that was accepted with gracious tolerance. She carried him away, whispering into his ear, her arms clasped around his tummy, his head next to hers, his four legs sticking out in front of them.

"My mother," said Deva, without preamble, "made a better story for me. She said my father was an American, who had come to help the people in that wretched place. She said she was lonely and scared in a rough town. She said that you were lonely too, and that you sought her out because you saw that she was one of the few decent people there. You wanted to help and protect her, and she believed your work was good, and perhaps dangerous. She said that in spite of you being older, you had loved each other thoughtfully and willingly, as equals.

That's what she said. She said she was worried that you too, like my grandfather, might be lost in the forest trying to help people. She said you were an exceptional and marvelous man, a hero, and that I should be proud to have you as a father. That's what she told me. She didn't say you raped her, then abandoned us. She died when I was thirteen, before I was adult enough to question her more closely. I wasn't a good daughter towards the end. I let her down in a terrible way. I am no better than you. Later, it was thoughts of you that made me want to go to America to study and make my life. I had some idea I might find you there.

"Instead, I found another American to get a Brazilian girl pregnant. People didn't think much of the American I chose. He was a heroin addict. But I knew he was good, and I loved him. I believe that my mother loved you the same way. I think that she really believed that you were a good man. My mother was a good judge of people."

Deva paused and gave John a cool look. "So, I'm going to choose to trust my mother's memory, not yours. I'm going to believe that even though she was only sixteen, she loved you, and that you did not rape her. Not really. I think maybe there was confusion and emotion, and that she was too young and you were too old, and that the politics there poisoned every- thing. Probably, it should not have happened. But I've been in the world enough to know that messy things happen. They are commonplace, and it is a fool who apportions blame with any confidence. I think there was love there, real love, and that was enough. That's what I choose to think. That's what I am choosing to believe. I don't know why she might have said what she did, but I know I've done and said some things crazy things in the heat of the moment, and I'll take my own nature to be my mother's. And she didn't run from you after, did she? You put her on a bus, and you were both in tears to separate. That's what she told me. Do you remember that? I remember it as clearly as if it was my own memory. I don't believe she was lying. I choose to believe that she remembered accurately, and that my memory of her telling me is also accurate. I choose to overlay her version on yours. What I think is that you felt dirty because you were ashamed of your work, America's work, and you chose a version of your relationship that expressed your shame. She only remembered you as good. And then you tried to do good, didn't you? Earthquake relief in Pakistan, and so on. The 'disaster expert,' as you put it. So, I'm choosing to be my mother. Who loved you. That's what was decided while I was asleep. Harry put me to sleep and I felt loved. I slept and my dreams were shaped by love. When I woke up, it was decided: I was going to love you. I was going to have a father."

John thought back. It was thirty-five years earlier, and it was all mixed up with so much he wanted to forget. Deva was right, there had been more to it. They had been tender together immediately afterwards. Yes, Veronica had even laughed once or twice. Genuine laughter, as he now recalled it, laughing at the both of them, and this unexpected thing that had happened between them. He could remember that now. He asked, "What did Veronica die of?"

"Cancer. She was only twenty-nine. Still beautiful, by the way."

"I'm so sorry." In the silence that followed, Deva came into the room and sat still on the end of the bed, looking at John, while he looked away. Finally, he turned towards her and asked, "Deva, how is that we're here together now? The two of us here in this house, so far away in time and place."

She shook her head. "I don't know. Harry found you. There's a lot I don't understand. I think perhaps Harry is capable of miracles."

Now there was a cascade of hurrying footsteps coming down the corridor that turned out to be Harry, pursued by Sunny, who was pursued by Nadia.

"Sunny loves Harry," Nadia declared breathlessly.

And so it seemed. The puppy was dogging Harry's steps, and Harry was smiling a wide smile containing a hint of mischief that John had not seen before. It was as if everything was going tremendously well, and Harry was tremendously delighted at how well everything was going. There was a new animation to him: Harry in charge; Harry being useful.

Nadia said, "Sunny knows where everyone is, and knows all about us. He just knows. Harry told me."

Harry now said, petting Sunny and not looking up, "John, you've spent too much time in your room. Let's all have tea and play a game of something. Don't you agree, Deva? Nadia, you can decide what we play."

While Nadia thought about this, John studied Deva's face until at last he saw her accede. "Why not?" She shrugged.

When it happened, and then happened again, the lovemaking was slow. Harry did not wish to shorten or alter the experience by pushing towards a finish, an approach with which Deva conspired by holding herself at bay. It was the best love she had known. Harry relaxed into her completely, quite unlike that other insistent man she knew from their other first night, and unlike any man she had ever known. He resided inside her, content to lodge his attention there, tracking their small movements, holding still, holding back, at the same time kissing, mouths fully available to each other, loving above, loving below, stopping for air at times and smiling at each other, then falling again into blind comfort, eyes closed, exquisite attention paid to the other's touch. There was no other destination, no intention of an ending, no intention of any sort. There was no forgetting in it, and no remembering. For the first time for a long time, Deva was able to dwell in the lovemaking, neither outside it, nor lost to it, but entirely conscious, entirely present, entirely free of the past.

Underneath Harry, she lifted her knees to squeeze his hips, keeping him close, then made them both topple sideways, on their sides, and by mutual agreement giving the balance of their attention to their mouths so that their lower movements would not defeat them with too much achievement. Deva understood that, in spite of her experience and the many compliments on her skills, she might not have been a very good lover, and nor had her most accomplished partners been good lovers. She could make a man come, and could make sure that she came too. She could take a man deep into her mouth and knew how to massage a prostate for extra effect. She could wind up her orgasms to the point of oblivion with the right toy and a durable man. She had tied men up and been tied up, had delivered hurt and been hurt; but what she had not experienced before—when fucking to be high, or fucking to obliterate, or to not be alone, or to just get it done—was to be alive in sex, to take the time to attend the man inside her, to learn to not move at all and explore that extraordinary stasis, everything offered, nothing taken. She had never before in her sexual life, which had started in Rio with Manuel pushing into her, let herself become sex like this, not imagining anyone but the person she was with, not needing to think of love because she was love.

Harry was not conscious of offering any special gift. His ease came easily. The attention to the changing pleasures of Deva, the gorgeous invitation of her, his wish to dwell there, came naturally. Time was unlimited; why would he want this to end when, by paying attention to Deva, he could live entirely in the world of Deva, her breasts pressed against him, her bottom in the palm of his hand, the light coming through the honeyed curtains shading the curve of her. Why would he want this to end, when at the end, there was thought, and the agitation of thought searching for memory?

The curtains were still closed from Deva's afternoon visit. The slanted light of dusk made a rolling landscape of the rumpled duvet. Harry lay there, half-covered, happy. Deva had gone with John and Sunny to meet Nadia from school. For once, he did not feel the lack of a greater purpose. Happiness did not require it. He smiled at himself to recall that he once imagined his mission might be to save the world.

He dozed, making a friend of sleep, which made a friend of wakefulness. His old sleep was a darker, deeper thing, an answer to the brain's complaint that too much consciousness was pain.

Into this undefended state two vagrant fragments of memory drifted into Harry's view and resolved themselves. They were of a type, both looking down upon a scene. In the first, the vantage point was a rocky outcrop on the hillside of a valley cut into a vast landscape, layers of snow-capped peaks in the distance. The scene below was a cluster of flat-roofed mud-brick houses barely differentiated from their earth of origin. There was a cow on the flat roof of one of the houses, attached to a central pivot by a pole, and walking in circles, though in the picture all movement was suspended. A woman in green robes squatted nearby holding a stick to encourage the cow. There was a sense of wonder and the feeling that something in this was forbidden. Lower down the valley, there were green fields and trees bordering the course of a river. He thought it was a scene from childhood, though it might as well have been a picture.

The second scene was also a view from above. In this case he was looking down from the edge of a sea cliff on shining blue water. Again, he appeared to be alone, and again, nothing moved. At the bottom left of the picture a stone mole unfurled from the shore out into the sea to make a little harbor, but there were no boats moored within its protective arm. While the first picture was of a wild place, this time his feet were set in a manicured garden of shrubs, succulent plants, and rocks. He was a man, not a boy, and although the scene was bright, it was overshadowed by care. The sun shining on the blue water should have been enchanting, but it produced no joy.

The two scenes presented themselves for inspection, then slipped away from him, evading further interrogation. They had been offered as clues, and he had failed to come up with the right questions to address them. He was left with the memory of memories.

I was beginning to think," Dr Elliot said to Deva and John, "that we were making no progress. I was wondering if we were spending Harry's money wisely having both of you here. Frankly, not doing all that much. Not that I can entirely blame you. It was never entirely clear what should be done. But these memories are promising. Thank you, Deva. Perhaps your new relationship with Harry shifted something, do you think?"

Deva had not told him of her new relationship with Harry, but Dr Elliot continued without any attempt to dissemble. "I was worried that too much vigor could set him back. I was going to say something to you, to hold back on the gymnastics, but it seems you might have accidentally caused a useful shift in something. Still, the warning stands. Do you have any thoughts on what he was seeing?"

While Deva gathered herself from this casual commentary on her intimate life, John spoke: "Not really. He hasn't any idea himself. Mountains. Sea. He thinks he might have been a child in the mountains. It sounded like a poor village somewhere."

"Deva?"

"I don't know. How would I?"

"Well, you were employed to pick up cultural cues, I believe."

"And because I'd slept with him. Remember?"

"No matter. Is there anything at all that suggests why these memories might be of particular significance? Some connection between them?"

"Nothing I can think of," said Deva. "Unless it's anxiety."

Dr Elliot waited for more and when it did not come, settled for, "Very well. Keep paying attention. Now, I want you to listen to what I'm going to say. It's very likely that these pictures are the first harbingers of a progressive return of his memory. A breakthrough, if you like. That's my prediction. Now, if Harry's brain has been holding memories back for self-protection, the return of memory implies danger to him. You understand? We can't say exactly what sort of trauma is involved. So, two things. Firstly, he must be kept very calm. Secondly, you must be ready to pay extra close attention to everything he says and does. Everything. And you will need to report to me more regularly. Similarly, I will examine Harry more often."

Dr Elliot looked from Deva to John then back to Deva, who started to speak, then stopped herself. "Very good," he continued. "Now one possibility is that his brain will over-excite itself trying to make sense of these first memories. It will search around, frantically looking for connections. It will try to build islands of memory around the new memories and then will try to join up the islands to make a coherent narrative. The mind wants to create order, even where none exists. That's the most likely scenario. The effort can be distressing. Probably earlier memories will appear first and then those closer to the moment of trauma will arrive later on. He may never be able to recall the actual car crash. It's also possible that the mind's wish to make sense out of the past will lead to the construction of questionable memories to create the illusion of coherence. I want you to keep note of everything. It's time for you to earn your keep."

Deva said, "He's happy now, you know. He's happy not trying too hard to remember."

"Harry's welfare is, of course, our priority. But the situation is intrinsically unstable. Now things have started to move, there is no going back. And making him happy in the way you make him happy, Deva, rather stretches your job description. Finally, he's a rich man and he's a vulnerable man. We are concerned about ethics here. There can't be any appearance of abuse."

Deva stared at Dr Elliot. She had never liked him. "Well, you'll have to ask Harry if he feels abused. I think he'll tell you he feels loved. And happy. As far as I know those are good for one's health."

"Harry is a severely injured patient in our care. He is not a fully responsible person. Frankly, my greatest concern at this time is that the shock of returning memory should not over-whelm him and cause him to regress. He can always slip back into a coma again. Or worse. I'll be bringing in a psychologist to help him process returning memories. Be attentive, but not too curious. And not…vigorous. The sexual intimacy should probably stop."

With lowered brows signifying her intense displeasure, Deva looked over at John, who raised his hand slightly, counseling restraint. Deva stood, containing her feelings. "Is that all?"

"For now. Thank you, Deva. We'll speak again tomorrow. John, a word, if you will."

With Deva gone, Dr Elliot relaxed back in his chair and was comfortably silent before turning to give John a wry look. "She won't stop of course. But that's okay. Quite a handful, your daughter."

"You know about that?"

"We monitor. It would be irresponsible not to. You're in the monitoring business yourself."

John said nothing. Then he decided on the anodyne, "Well, yes, you have to be careful."

"What do you think, John? Could that first picture be Pakistan? The tribal areas? You've been there recently."

"Could be. Or a thousand other places."

"Let's say for the sake of argument that it is. Would you make any connections with the second memory?"

"What sort of connections?"

"Political, for example. With anything you know yourself."

"Nothing's occurred to me. There's not much to go on."

"Then I ask you to keep working on it. And keep a close eye on Deva too."

"My daughter."

"Yes, quite the surprise that, wasn't it?"

"For me, it was. How did you know I've been in Pakistan recently?"

Dr Elliot looked mildly taken aback. "Our mutual friends. Come on, you're an old hand. You never get to stop being an old hand. When you travel, someone gives permission. That applied to coming here, didn't it? Someone signed off."

"If you say so," said John. "And now your cards are on the table, what is it you want from me exactly?"

"Keep a close eye on Deva. For her own good. She's emotionally involved and therefore unpredictable. Otherwise, of course, we want what Washington wants, the same as your friend Gwen wants. We want to stop people on our side dying in terrorist attacks. Harry knows something. He's connected. He was going to do something. And to that end, no mercy. His memory is coming back. Some memories have escaped. It's time to crack him open."

"What about all these fears of relapse and the dangers of overstimulation. Being gentle, and so on."

"We're done with it, really. Time's up. There's an opportunity and we're throwing the dice."

"It's not what you told Deva."

"Deva's on the outside. You're on the inside. I hope there's no confusion there. Any problem?"

"How to go about it? The cracking. You're the psychiatrist. The pro."

"Neurologist, technically. As to how you do it, I'd say, why not tell him what you saw in Pakistan? Let him process that. That might be a start."

John nodded, said nothing.

"You need to stay very alert, John. Harry will not be the same person when his memory comes back. God knows what he'll be."

Later that day, John asked Deva if he might help give Nadia her bath, and perhaps then read something to her. "Of course," said Deva. "She'll love that."

In the bathroom, the taps running, the two of them bending over together to whip up the bubbles for Nadia, John said, "Deva, I talked more with Dr Elliot and I want you to listen carefully. The situation is this. Harry is a Pakistani and he's a prisoner here in his own house. They think he's a terrorist, or knows something about terrorists. That's the only reason they care about his memory. Dr Elliot is British intelligence. Mrs. Slater too. They trust me to a degree, but they don't trust you at all. They don't care anything about Harry except finding out what he knows. And they're willing to destroy him to find out. So, it's up to us to care about Harry, isn't it? They think I'm with them, but I'm not. I'm done with all that. It's poisoned my life. I'm with you. And I'm with Harry. Look what he's given us. You understand? We're pawns in whatever this is. I haven't worked out exactly what. But I think they already knew you were my daughter, and didn't tell us. The house is monitored, so this is the only place we can talk, and then only like this with our heads down over the bath and the water running. Please trust me on this, Deva. Please just trust me. Will you?"

Deva looked into John's earnest face. "You're my father," she said.

Harry sat quietly in the little suntrap garden where the others rarely went. He liked it there, and had decided to inhabit it. Eventually he would bring Nadia there. And Deva. He did not like the doctor's instruction not to make love to Deva and was thinking that he would ignore it. Such was the meandering of his mind when his defenses fell.

Memories appeared from afar like migrating birds determined to reach their destination.

Recollections of childhood came first and most easily, the women in the household—his mother, grandmother, aunts, his older sister, Samina—warm and present. He was in bed at home, unwell—a difficulty with breathing—an illness of early childhood that kept him away from the company of boys and men and the greater world. They came easily now, these most distant of memories, echoes of his present convalescent life.

His mind worked first on the reconstruction of those early days, his bedroom in Peshawar, his other bedroom in the mountains, and the walled garden in the compound there. He lay there in summer, the sun burning through the thin mountain air, a stream tinkling in his ears. It was a paradise, in spite of the poor health that led him to it. In scenes from later childhood, the asthma was gone, replaced by strength and attention to the ways of men, as if his body had dismissed it, along with other childish things, weakness, and the company of women.

Harry's mind lingered in those early memories from Pakistan, the details filling in, liking, apparently, its residence in remote times. He urged it to advance towards the present. For now, there were these memories of his childhood in Pakistan and there was today, this house in London. He called for markers from between.

In reluctant obedience, as if the instruction was an imposition, and perhaps unwise, his brain complied, establishing little outposts in the troublesome years of nine, ten, eleven, when the family was afflicted with worries about the war against the Soviets. His middle brother, Akbar, was off with the mujahedin, and the older, Ibrahim, was already busy with the business of transporting heroin to Karachi.

His father's face was darkened in these memories, troubled by the hectic pulls of the war, the newly abrasive religious authorities, the dangers and moral complication of the drug trade, the protection and unity of his people, the intrusion of Pakistani intelligence agents, and behind them, pulling strings, always the Americans and their geopolitical games, hexing the villagers' more ancient game against nature: growing food enough to survive in a climate and landscape inhospitable to the attempt. Harry remembered his father's worried face. He was a good man in one of the world's least touched places, yet tormented even there by the tearing Cold War pulls of Moscow and Washington. There were long family discussions, his mother counseling for all things quiet and prudent.

In the village, there was from time to time, a conspicuous visitor, an American, his father's friend. It was John. Harry was nearly sure. It was a younger John. Apparently, he had known John all his life. He had watched him when spying through the flap of a tent, while John talked with a circle of tribal elders in the high mountains. John was the wonder in that tent, younger than the youngest elder, and the only one not bearded. He wore a shirt and tight trousers, and looked uncomfortable sitting crossed-legged in front of the spread of delicacies filling the rug between the men. The importance of the occasion was sufficient to be marked by a feast, from which the young Harry—Zamir then—had been excluded.

There were other sightings. John was talking with his father in the outer room of their house where the men from other families were received. John and his father were on horseback, returning exhausted and newly bonded from a difficult mountain journey. John had been the exotic shadow passing through Harry's childhood, always welcome, always kept separate, the only one of his type ever seen in the village. He was his father's special American, under his father's protection. When the two of them met over tea in the reception room, they talked for hours, and it had seemed to Harry that his father enjoyed those conversations, patched together in a mixture of English and Urdu, and that there was sometimes laughter, a very rare thing. But, of course, John would not know today that watchful small boy in the background, not old enough then to play any part. But it also came to Harry that there had been another, later meeting. In a city. New York. His father had taken the family to New York for pleasure, and John, an older John, had come to meet them. They had all gone to a restaurant, one that John had chosen, and there had been reminiscences about earlier times, more difficult times, times definitively past, when the men had shared some battles. The battles were all won now, and could be savored. Harry's family was prosperous and respectable in this memory, and Afghanistan was at peace. Harry was the schoolboy visiting from England, still nothing to John, he supposed.

It went this way, returning memory: a little impression of unlabeled place and time, a few pictures establishing it, then a filling in to make a density of existence, then a darting to some new time and place to establish another foothold, then reason interrogating the space between, to make a map of it. In this way, village memories induced the memory of John, then hopped to New York, then had hopped back to Harry's boarding school in England, then to a visit to Samira in Oxford, and then on to the London house—this house where he now sat—busy and noisy with all the family from Pakistan. Playing cricket—yes—playing with his friend Mohammed, the only other Pakistani in his year at the expensive school, though they would never have been close in Pakistan. Harry—Zamir—was the son of a tribal leader made rich through the American war and opium, and Mohammed was the son of an elite family with

a distinguished history of government service, his father the
Permanent Secretary of a ministry. But they were in England,
and they were free.

Harry could not manufacture a picture of Mohammed at
university. That was a different crowd. The name of it, the
name of the university? Yes, East Anglia. He was with an arty,
political crowd, learning to drink and smoke pot, discovering his
talent for poetry, and losing his virginity to a more experienced
and cute-in-her-glasses twenty-year-old, for whom corrupting
Harry was an intriguing transgression, he a virgin, a Moslem,
a Pakistani. That memory came back, a smile with it. He had
lived a life. And he had moved to London. After university, he
moved to London. There was the shared house in Tufnell Park,
his housemates there. A series of girlfriends—Elizabeth, Claire,
Brigit—all nice, educated girls. He had been a poet, a serious
poet. The past was filling in. The man in Tufnell Park was not
so different from the man he was now, the time not so long ago.
But there remained a gap that resisted completion, a forbidding
emptiness between the then and now.

When the advance of memories from the past stalled, Harry
tried instead to work backwards from the present. He started
with Deva. He had known Deva before the accident, but she
had not yet appeared in his memories. She had told him that
they met at a nightclub and finally Harry was delivered an image
that seemed to fit: Deva on a brightly lit stage. He was away
from it, in shadow, his back against a wall. There were tables
and people between him and Deva, great impediments. She was
in the light, smiling, bowing, being applauded, making graceful gestures of appreciation. Deva glowing. A star. And from
there? From there? They had met later, Deva had said. Here
she was, in the booth with him. They were talking. They were
strangers, not friends. Wary. Harry was anxious, full of conflict-
ing feelings. There was something terribly wrong. It did not feel
the way it felt with Deva now. It was not love and ease. He was
somewhere else with her, and he was troubled. A bedroom.

Deva had said nothing of this. Where was this coming from? This was Deva's home. They were lovers, then. He was making love to Deva and it was all wrong, all wrong in his head. It was nothing like their recent lovemaking. He was hating himself. Resenting her. Excited by Deva and resenting her. Enjoying the tenderness, and hating himself for enjoying it. Yes...because he also wanted to harm her. Sickeningly, he had been thinking about harming Deva. He was taking comfort from her while thinking of how to hurt her, a scratchy push-pull love. Why such madness?

Harry was in a large air-conditioned office, sitting across from Mohammed. His old friend from the public school in Hertfordshire was a grown man in this picture. So, Mohammed had been back in his life more recently. They were no longer boys. And the big office was a Pakistani office, meaning that Mohammed was someone important in Pakistan since it was certainly his office and not Harry's. A peon, a clerk, had just come in to serve them tea and biscuits. A few minutes earlier, the peon had been summoned by the electric bell on the underside of Mohammed's desk. It all added up to Mohammed being a high official in Pakistan, and Harry his guest. Deva was not there of course. She had never been to Pakistan, and had met him only once in the past, at the Miranda nightclub, including the continuation of that night at her flat, which she had never mentioned.

Deva was not in the office, but her name was in the office. She was somehow connected. There was the same complicated feeling as when he had first made love to her, or at least one was a shadow of the other. This came first, this meeting in the office. Dark feelings. The idea of hurting Deva was here.

John's name was also present. Harry's memories of Deva were somehow leading to John. It was John who was the subject of the conversation between himself and Mohammed, and was also the subject of the cardboard file in the middle of the desk, tied up with string in the old civil service way, and generously stamped with red capitals, faded to pink, declaring all possible

tiers of secrecy. Harry was the petitioner in this picture, asking
something of his old friend, who had, like his father before
him, risen to somewhere high in government service. Secret
stuff. Intelligence. Mohammed was being kindly, patient. He
was showing Harry sympathy and respect. There was the tea
and biscuits, the unhurried allocation of time, the closed office
door. Mohammed was gently explaining something in a soft
voice. He was using Harry's childhood name, Zamir, making
it personal. He was explaining to his friend Zamir that there
was a short story or a long story. If he gave Zamir the short
story, it would be more general, and would not require Zamir
to do anything. Also, the short story, by being more general,
was more true, less prone to mistakes. The longer story was
likely to involve specific people, times and places that, given
the strict honor code of Zamir's people, might imply a need for
action, though any action taken could prove to be misplaced,
even perhaps a grievous error. Mohammed urged Zamir to
think about this carefully, and to favor the shorter story. If he
chose the shorter story, which essentially elaborated the general
proposition that America was to blame for everything, he could
return, untroubled, to his life in London. Honor would not
require of him a specific action for so general a story. On the
other hand, if specific people were invoked, as they could be
in a longer version, he would be unable to escape the inflexible
Puktunwari requirement for revenge, which was rightly respect-
ed and feared throughout the world. And in truth, though
Mohammed did not challenge the authority of the old ways
that had served them so well, it might create greater difficulties
for Mohammed if Zamir made use of information obtained
from him to commit some awful act of diplomatic significance
because of a faulty understanding. So, though the gravity of the
offence now being answered would not let him refuse Zamir's
request for information, wouldn't he rather stay with the shorter story, the truer one, really, of long history and global forces
and their customary collateral misery?

Harry hoped that memory would reveal him taking

Mohammed's advice and show him walking from the office, free from the darkness that surrounded him there, but it could not. It showed him instead insisting on the longer story and Mohammed conceding that, given the enormity of the offence to Zamir, and the bonds of tradition and friendship, he could not refuse.

Then there was John's name in Mohammed's mouth. John Bradley, the old friend of Zamir's father going back decades. Mohammed tapped the file to indicate its deep sediment. Did Zamir know John Bradley had recently returned to Pakistan to visit Zamir's father? Did Zamir remember the American from his childhood? Zamir thought he did. Well, explained Mohammed, that was John Bradley. He had not been to Pakistan for decades, but three weeks earlier he suddenly returned to visit Zamir's father, who was, what, about eighty-five? Zamir confirmed his father's age. Quite a coincidence, the timing, Mohammed noted. Your father gave him all the hospitality due to an old and trusted friend. He took him to your village. No American had been able to go up there for a very long time. It followed that John Bradley would have known of the wedding preparations for Zamir's brother, Akbar. It's all in here, Mohammed said, tapping the file again. Everything we know about him from the 1980s up to now. Even his career before he first came to Pakistan. There's the earthquake relief, the war against the Soviets, his personal life—all sorts of things. Mohammed opened the file and picked up the top sheet, a paper not yet browned, and looked at it. For example, he said, John Bradley has an illegitimate daughter from Brazil about whose existence he is ignorant. Yet in the curious way the intelligence world works, we know about her, here in Pakistan. It seems the Americans considered her a security issue from the time her mother first approached their consulate in Brazil. There is also something here about her asking questions in Washington. Apparently, she had the son of an American senator for a lover. Now she was in London and might be of interest to Zamir, he supposed. A nightclub singer.

Goes by the name of Deva. John Bradley himself was back living peacefully in the American countryside. New Hampshire. The details were here. He was long estranged from his family. This Deva might be the most potent instrument for the equality of damage that was Zamir's right.

In the old days, Mohammed explained, there was a common trust with the Americans. They shared intelligence, including details of their operatives in Pakistan. That was when they were allies fighting the Russians in Afghanistan. Not so much now. Now the Pakistanis did their own intelligence, and he had made sure that the file was up-to-date. Bradley's recent visit had necessitated it. Intelligence types, Mohammed observed, do not retire. Then he closed the file and explained that, unfortunately, he could not show Zamir anything in the file, because it was, of course, top secret, and if Zamir did by any chance come to know of anything that was in the file, then it must by definition have come from some other source. However, he did at that moment have a pressing need to go to the toilet, and because he was leaving a sensitive file on his desk, he would need to lock the office with Zamir in it while he was gone. If he didn't mind. He might be gone some time.

Harry was Zamir in this memory, and there was darkness in him. The reason was close now, held only just beyond his knowledge. And there it was: an explosion, overwhelming and sickening, the long-resisted destination of his unforgetting.

The key was another shard of memory, a third scene looked down upon from a higher place, the third member of its genus. This was not the puzzle of the bright blue sea, or a childhood view of a cow on a roof. Those first two memories had been harmless offerings, mere clues to the existence of this third. They had been offered as substitutes for it, or leads to it.

In this third scene from above, Harry had recently abandoned a family gathering and was looking down on it. The preparations for the wedding of Akbar were under way, and

Harry did not like any of it. There had been too many questions from relatives about his life in London, and especially about why he was not married. That his middle brother was marrying again was also notable, but then the life he led, first with the mujahedin and now with the Taliban in Afghanistan, explained much, and excused all. The wedding had brought with it more religion, more family, and more ceremony than Harry could bear. He had not been home for twenty years and no one present could conceive of how he was changed or that he no longer belonged there. He had no sympathy with the Taliban's vicious intolerance. He did not think Akbar's sacrifices were admirable. In turn, the life he had made in London meant nothing to these people. It was unimaginable to them, and therefore worthless. Any admiration for his poetry in London was admiration from people whose opinion counted for less than nothing.

Excitement was growing around his brother's imminent arrival, both for the occasion of the wedding and because Akbar's arrivals were rare, unpredictable, and always accompanied by all the subterfuge and drama of the protection required for a senior Taliban. While Harry was reckoned a failure, Akbar was a cherished celebrity. Harry had walked away from the commotion and up a steep mountain path above the village. He had done this as a child, but this time he was a man and he went higher. The snow was melted and the spring flowers were out, sparse, hardy little flowers in blue, white, and yellow. He had a notebook in his hand and wanted to find the calm of a poem in all this, wanted to rediscover himself. Solitude was easier to find in London than in his mountain home.

He climbed high above the valley until the loudest sound was the breeze moving among the plants. The air was pure and the day was clear. Some of the world's highest peaks stretched out to the north, glistening white. He had forgotten: this was also paradise. The valley below was jeweled with bright green farms, strung together alongside the silver of a snowmelt river. British colonizers had compared the region to Switzerland, though Switzerland was much the lesser. He breathed more slowly and deeply. He should be happy for his austere brother, that he was marrying again, and would have the comfort of family to set against the long stress of fighting against invaders. The effort had, after all, started as a worthy cause, and who was he to judge? A hawk made effortless circles overhead, a perfect sunny day to be lifted by air currents from the warming rock, bad news for its little mammalian prey. Harry opened his notebook, hoping to discover something small and valuable in himself to set against the turbulent sociability he had left below. The tiny figures of relatives and other clan members were visible in the family compound and gathered on the track outside. His brother was to be married to a cousin, in accordance with tradition. Reportedly, he had arrived just this morning from Afghanistan, overland, and deliberately last minute. Harry had flown into Islamabad the day before, direct from London, and was driven straight to the mountains and the besieging attention of his relatives. The speed of the transition from sitting in the crowded Tube to Heathrow to balancing on this quiet, sunlit mountainside was shocking.

The buzzing sound, when it first registered with him, was faint and distant. It was shifting and hard to locate, rising and falling in volume, then rising more, until it finally had Harry's attention as something approaching and man-made. Not an insect. He looked down. There was a white Land Cruiser followed by a pick-up making its way down the narrow track cut into the side of the mountain, the only route down from the pass. That would be his father's Land Cruiser, with his parents and brothers arriving for the ceremony, together with his sister and her husband. The pick-up, packed with armed men, would be Akbar's escort. He should climb back down to welcome them. But the cars were too far below to be a credible source for the sound, and in any case, it was the wrong sound. It was the sound of summer Sundays in Hertfordshire, the local flying club amateurs in their little propeller planes—something for a schoolboy to look up for and enjoy. Then he saw it, white in the sun, a tiny, long-winged plane, a toy, far above him. He knew all about the drones, of course, that they were an omnipresent terror in life here—mostly watching, sometimes killing; no one could tell which and when—but this was the first he had seen for himself. It was tracing the curve of the valley below with an efficient steadiness. The drone was a small, slow thing compared to the thunderous, roaring Soviet jets that had terrified him when he was a child. It struck him first as more charming than threatening, much as a tiger might for an instant be noted as graceful before it leapt upon its observer.

In spite of the unhurried steadiness of its progress, the drone soon arrived, circled, and with little fuss or hesitation, unburdened itself of a missile, which, with a direct, no-nonsense trajectory, hit the Land Cruiser in an intense explosion, followed quickly by a second missile, which disposed of the pick-up. The explosions left nothing to doubt: white flash turning instantly to red, framed for a moment by black smoke, then everything expanding at a rush, the noise and force hitting him, dust and smoke storming up the mountainside until they curled acridly around his legs. There could be no doubt, yet he hoped for doubt. His family could not have survived, yet they must have survived. They had changed their plans and had not been in the car; the explosions were more show than substance; the car would be revealed intact. He was running now, slip-sliding down the mountainside. The drone meandered, pristine, in the sunlight—human hands had polished it—at first going away, then loitering as the dust settled to check on the completeness of its work, before its final diminishment to speck.

The route Harry took down the mountain should have killed him with its dangerous directness, but he was possessed at the time of exceptional abilities. He reached the bottom and ran towards the heat of the twisted, burned-out vehicles. People were reeling, screaming. Some who had been closer were lying dead, some were alive but wounded. A man, an old uncle, once a childhood favorite, was horribly injured, but astonishingly still upright, an arm ripped from him—a squirter—looking confused and beseeching, as if Harry might possess his missing arm. Of his immediate family, there was nothing left. It later proved difficult to find pieces to bury.

This, then, was the destination of his returning memories. Harry had seen all his family killed in front of his eyes, all who he had loved the best and longest.

On a more distant hill, John asked the driver to stop on their winding route through the mountains on their way back to Islamabad airport. He stepped out of the car to look back towards the distant village that had been an important and honorable part of his life. His friend was old, and John was also ageing. He did not expect to return. He was pleased to have come.

John did not see the drone coming. He was too far away. The explosion erupted in the center of a gaze that was unfocused while thoughts and emotions were playing in him. It was small and bright, then larger and red, then big and black with smoke. This was the third of the blooms that had come to him while picking daffodils, after the other two horrors of his life. He looked urgently. He could not be sure the explosion was exactly at the village he had just left. The explosion was only somewhere in its vicinity. His immediate instinct was to tell the driver to return there urgently. But almost as immediately he understood that he had no place there. Indeed, the driver was shouting urgently that he should return to the vehicle so that they could distance themselves further. The driver was panicked, fearing that they too might be in danger. And John also understood that he dare not go back to the village because in all likelihood, without any intention on his part, he had led the drone to its target, and that, in all likelihood, his friend and all his family were now dead because of him. In all likelihood, he had been used. He could not bear to know for sure.

arry does it better," Nadia asserted to Deva and John at some point in their game.

"Where is Harry?" Deva asked. "I didn't see him go to bed. Nadia, why don't you go and find him?"

John, whose acting in Nadia's fantasy life fell short of Harry's standard, said, "Yes, tell him we need him. We need Ming."

Harry was not in his room, Nadia reported back, which created a mystery. "I'll go look for him," she said, and skipped off down the hallway, Sunny in pursuit, skittering faster than his motor skills and the slippery floor allowed.

Deva and John watched the skipping girl and her tumbling pup, then fell into a shared laughter, father and daughter laughing together, then suddenly becoming aware of it. Deva, not wanting any words, hugged John and kissed him on the cheek, causing a dopey smile on a face unpracticed with dopey smiles.

The little sun garden with its plants imported from distant deserts was not on any of the customary routes through the house. Nadia flew through hallways, opening and closing doors in full proprietary confidence, a treasure hunt. But it was Sunny, with a nose and love to direct him, who found Harry sitting on a stone bench in the garden, his eyes closed. Sunny put his front paws on Harry's shins and scratched at him, whimpering.

"Harry!" Nadia called out imperiously on seeing him, then, "Harry!" again as she came closer, now perplexed at his stillness, but thinking that most likely this was a game in which Harry would at any moment burst forth to frighten her and make her giggle. "Harry, don't be silly," she said, extending a single finger to poke him in the shoulder to no effect. Then she backed away and cried out, "Mamie! Mamie!" turning to run.

Deva and John bent over him. "He's breathing," said John. "His pulse is okay. Maybe a bit slow."

"Harry," Deva breathed into his ear, wanting to communicate as directly as possible with his brain.

"He's not asleep," said John. "I think it's something else. He's cold."

"Harry," whispered Deva again, urging him to hear her. Then, as if instructed to summon her most potent powers, she brought her lips to his lips. Not passionately, but sealing her lips against his, breathing her breath into his mouth, and taking his back into hers.

His lips moved minutely in proof of life, and Deva pulled away. She took a tissue and wiped his cheeks. He had been crying. He opened his eyes. They were not quite the familiar eyes. "Harry, are you all right?" she asked.

He did not reply immediately and Deva looked to John for help, who positioned himself in front of Harry, looking into the unblinking gaze. "Maybe a stroke," he murmured to Deva. He held up three fingers. "Harry, how many fingers am I holding up?"

Harry gathered an attention to the blur of fingers, then slowly moved his focus to John's face.

"Can you speak, Harry? Do you know my name?"

Harry nodded slowly. "You're John Bradley."

"Good. Deva, we should get him to bed."

"Should we call Mrs. Slater?"

"Not yet."

Deva had draped herself over Harry's body, urging her warmth into him. "I love you, Harry," she said. "We all love you." Harry moved his eyes from John's face to Deva's face, his expression blank.

John said, "Okay, let's get him to bed. At least he's not gone into a coma." Then, "Come on, Harry, can you stand?" He put his arm around him, and heaved him up so that, with Deva on his other side, they could stumble towards the bedroom.

Nadia was staring silently, scared by all this, and Deva set her to work. "Nadia, we need you to open the doors for us. Harry needs a nap."

Once in bed, his trousers removed—a leg apiece for Deva and John—Harry spoke. "It's all right," he said. "I need to sleep. My brain. ..." He managed a wan grimace. "...Too much... You can leave me now."

"What happened?" asked John.

"I remembered," said Harry, his eyes closing. There was no invitation in the statement.

John and Deva exchanged a glance, then Deva bent down to say, "Sleep!" and kissed Harry on the cheek. She moved away, drawing John and Nadia with her. "Don't you dare leave us again, Harry," she said. "Remember we love you. We're your family and we love you."

Harry echoed more quietly, "You're my family and I love you."

Dr Elliot was annoyed. "He was doing well. His memory was coming back. His interactions with you were normal, weren't they?"

"They were," confirmed John.

"And he said nothing about what he'd remembered?"

"Nothing. Only that he remembered."

"Did you tell him what you knew, John? Did you jog his memory? Ask about Pakistan?"

"I didn't have the chance."

"He said he loved us," said Deva. "And that we were his family."

A tic of irritation worked around Dr Elliot's mouth. "He was ready to talk and you didn't question him?"

"Harry was barely alive," said Deva. "You don't care about him at all."

"I staked my reputation on you two. Deva, please leave us."

After she was gone, Dr Elliot said, "John, you know Harry was at your house. The photograph? You're lucky to be alive. Now he's remembered something and he doesn't want us to know. He's trying to forget it. I think he's deliberately trying to shut his brain down again. That's what's happening in my view. And we don't want him to shut down, do we? Because we need to know."

"We?"

"We. You and me. And our various masters, of course. He wasn't at your house for a social call. So, yes, we."

"I thought I came here to help the son of an old friend. That was the assignment. Nothing more."

"We needed you to be convincing. It worked with your visit to Pakistan, didn't it? You were convincing then. The sincere friend. We were helping you to be convincing."

John thought about this. They assumed, no matter what they did, that he would be their man. Nothing was for Harry. Or Deva. Or him.

He stood and gripped the astonished Dr Elliot's head in his hands, bringing his own face very close, and said carefully and clearly, "Dr Elliot, I'm not your man."

Elliot, red-faced, shook himself free. "Right! Right. I'll pass that on. And whose man shall I say you are? America's man?"

"Try, family man."

"Meaning what? Oh, you think you have a little family here? You, Deva, Harry, the little girl. The puppy. Your Harry—that is, Zamir—was planning to kill you. That was his first mission."

John stood and looked at Dr Elliot, then smiled. "Well, that's families for you."

"You know why he was going to kill you?"

"I've an idea," said John, opening the door. "But then there are so many good reasons."

"Not just you. Your daughter too. That's what reconnected you. He was going to kill you both. For starters."

John closed the door behind him.

Harry was weak now. If memory made a human life, he did not want it. Memory was the end of happiness. His damaged brain preferred to close rather than suffer the upheaval of reordering emotion. He would not resist its further closing. John, who he loved, had caused his family to be killed. Except that this assertion collided with a certainty that John was not a murderous man. The John he knew was part of the happiness of others. Deva said that the memories we select make us who we are, and he would not choose bitter memories. The contradictions were too painful to be held inside an injured brain: he had set out to kill those whom he now loved best. This was why he had found them and come to know them. Helpfully, his brain was switching off the lights.

To the frustration of Dr Elliot, Harry slipped into unconsciousness with nothing more revealed. John and Deva sat by him in shifts, urging his return.

When Harry next surfaced, he found his hand in John's. Oblivion was not yet willing to take him. Memory was not yet fully done with him. He was in New Hampshire taking the photo of John picking a daffodil. He had gone to America to take revenge but was instead taking a photograph. Revenge was postponed.

His intention had been to punish the man now holding his hand. More than any anonymous soldier guiding a drone and scoring bug-splats from a comfy chair, this man was held responsible for the death of his family. Worse than any soldier, he had exploited his father's loyalty to do it. As unobtrusively as he could manage, Harry withdrew his hand from John's.

There was the mysterious sense of purpose with which he

had first emerged into consciousness. It was not to save the world, as he first imagined, nor even to mend Deva and John, as he came to think. His forgotten purpose was to take revenge by taking life.

Harry's determination to find Deva before dealing with John had gained force while he watched John in New Hampshire. The man was old. Harry saw a stiff old man picking flowers in the cold. He was not the vigorous American he recalled from childhood. This man was alone, vulnerable, concerned with flowers, lost in contemplation. This man needed a hat. He tried to feel the evil, but faltered in the attempt. He was not cut out for this.

The daffodils were beguiling. *A host, of golden daffodils.* Wordsworth's too familiar words came to him. Harry worked to rediscover the righteous anger that was kindled in Pakistan. He had sworn off alcohol and women, and stayed in Lebanon by the glittering sea while his anger was educated into resolve and strategy. This was the other shard of memory. He was standing in a garden in Lebanon, looking down on the sea, gathering himself there, consciously taking into himself the steel of purpose. He was the guest of old family friends, allies from the days when both Moslem families built their fortunes out of heroin. The family were arms dealers now, more or less respectable, holy benefactors.

In the cold of New Hampshire, Harry summoned the picture of his perplexed uncle, his arm missing. He imagined his mother, his father, his sister, Samira, together with his brothers, crowded and jostled in the Toyota, a wedding party, as the car rocked down the uneven track. They might have been joking together in the cozy interior, happy in their last moment.

Harry took a photo. At that instant, John tottered forward, then recovered himself, as if Harry had struck him. This was shocking, almost supernatural. He resolved to do nothing, but to return to London and find the daughter. After all, until John knew his daughter, he could not suffer the loss of her.

As Harry backed away into the woods, he saw John steady himself, shake his head to clear it, then reach down to cut the daffodil.

Only now, lying still in recollection, did it seem to Harry that something else was in play when he turned away. He did not trust what he was told in Pakistan. He slipped his hand back into John's, and said, "I'm going to close my eyes now, John. I know Deva and Nadia will be safe with you."

Harry was dying, and was dying willingly. Memory was dismissed. It flew from him as if it had never been. What was memory anyway? It was not something real. And look, here were the waving hands, beckoning him back, drawing him into their welcoming avenue. They were acclaiming him. A hero's return. He had, after all, done well, out there in the other world. He had got it right. He had no further need of life, and so let go of the last of it. It was a great relief. He fell into his true home.

There was no funeral for Harry. Men came in the night and took away his body. In the morning, the breakfast laid out for the three of them was sparse. Mrs. Slater informed them that it would be their last. With Harry gone, their jobs were finished. By tomorrow they must be gone. This was not their home. Mrs. Slater's tone was not deferential.

"We're Harry's friends," said Deva. "We want to stay for his funeral. Who else does he have?"

Mrs. Slater looked scornful. "Family only."

"What family?"

"I really can't say."

"Deva," said John, staying Deva's movement towards Mrs. Slater. "Leave her. She's nobody."

John thought he had all the pieces now. Harry was a terrorist suspect, and a well-connected potential resource, with family links to the Taliban, Pakistani intelligence, terrorist networks, and the tribal areas. A high-value asset, in their view. It was why Deva was here, and why he was here. He explained it to Deva: "We were bait for a fishing expedition. You were love and I was hate, brought in to stir up someone too fragile to interrogate. And it worked in a way. Except that Harry gave himself to us instead of them. That's how I see it. And they got our memories instead of his. Deva, we need to get out of here."

2020

John bent over to tie Sunny to the parking meter outside Omar's Bookshop Café. Sunny knew the routine. He sat to receive the rub behind his ears and then the treat that John retrieved from his coat pocket. "Stay here, boy," he told him unnecessarily. "Back soon." Sunny gave him a reproachful look, and flopped down with a dramatic sigh. He would be scoring some petting from passersby soon enough.

He no longer went to the gym every morning, nor did he buy the *New York Times*. Chores back at the farmhouse were exercise enough, and buying a paper made him look old-fashioned, he'd been told by Nadia. In any case, when would he have the chance to read it?

It was five years since they had left London. John's first visit to the café after his return was to meet Gwen. He had avoided her for a month.

"You were supposed to debrief," she told him.

"Nothing to tell. The man gave nothing away, then died."

"Not for you to decide."

"Oh, I disagree. I don't recall being employed for that assignment."

"Your expenses were paid."

"By Harry."

"We don't get to retire, John."

"Again, I disagree. I have. You could."

Gwen raised her long eyes across the café table and fixed him in her gaze. John found more tiredness in them than intimidation. The intelligence was undimmed. "I've protected you," she said. "You've brought the girl back with you. And the girl's girl."

"And the girl's girl's dog. We're speaking of my daughter, Deva. And my granddaughter, Nadia."

Gwen nodded. "Yes, indeed. They're going to leave you alone."

"Meaning?"

"The powers-that-be are going to leave you alone. As I said, I've protected you."

"Thank you. But why is that even necessary? What are they going to do? The powers-that-be don't have any loyalty and don't deserve ours. Look at you. You're going blind. You can barely walk. And you're running errands."

Gwen nodded. "Maybe I'll discover a long-lost child and find meaning for myself. But it doesn't work that way for women, does it? As to what they could do for you, and my protection. Well, your family is here, isn't it?"

"Right. They were allowed in. If that was you, thanks. I assumed they just wanted us out of London."

"It did suit them. Look, John, this is what I do. For as long as my brain is good and they find a use for me, I'll do it. It may all be shit, as you seem to think now. Perhaps it was always shit. But then, who of us knows what is and isn't? Maybe the historians in a hundred years when everything has played out. But probably not even then. You can't depend on virtue for doing right. Loyalty, though, that's available."

"Leaving aside only the question of to what, or whom."

For her first weeks in New Hampshire, Deva was lost to sadness, barely looking up, or around. John cooked and cared, and made sure Nadia was occupied, holding everything in place while waiting for Deva to return to them.

In all her life, Deva had never lingered in sadness. There had been hurt and anger, and mad activity, and promiscuity, and drugs. There had been a child to care for, the catharsis of singing, and the relief from feeling offered by intellect. But she had not known surrender. She had never been simply sad. With Harry, Deva had been loved, and had loved. She thought that such a pure, unselfish love could not be replaced.

The loss of Harry expanded in Deva to include her earlier

loss of Andy, her other gentle lover. There had been no room
for simple sadness then, with a baby coming and the agony of
withdrawal to live through. After that, Nadia had been there,
needing Deva to be healthy and able, depending on her for care
and protection. There had not been time to return to sadness
then. Harry's final unselfishness was to share the mourning of
himself with another. Those she loved most, Deva thought,
died. Her love was toxic, her allure as misleading as a daffodil's.
She thought darkly that her life had always been poisoned, that
it had been poisoned from its very conception. Her sadness
reached back to her mother, her beautiful mother who had died
while Deva was betraying her.

John brought food out to the garden seat where Deva spent
hours alone. Nadia brought her hugs, then returned to John and
his attention.

Finally, Deva mourned herself, the girl, unprotected by any
father, who at thirteen was unable to mourn her mother's death
for the fear that she was the cause of it. She had been abused,
she now allowed, reluctant still to surrender her agency. She
had taken drugs to answer a pain not of her own making. She
went with many men because she feared any one man. And she
had lost the first man who was safe enough for her to love, and
then the second. But she forced herself to acknowledge that
she had achieved much, in spite of all. And that she had a lovely
daughter. And that she had found a father.

The garden brought Deva back. She had never had a garden,
and John's efforts for his backyard had been more the resistance
of disorder than nurture. She saw the daffodils for herself, the
first and brightest moment in the year. Nothing sinister, after
all. Following which, she noticed that a disappointing dullness
set in. She already knew this piece of nature. She learned about
its soil, and vegetation and climate in the British Library. Deva
planted, ruined her nails, roiled the sadness in her, while nature
bled it from her. She came to understand why romantic poets
let the nature outside of them stand for the feelings inside.
She planted rhododendrons, honeysuckle, lilies, clematis,

hydrangeas, crocuses, tulips, bluebells, chrysanthemums, snow-drops, azaleas, and more. She went through the garden cata-logues and spent John's money freely. I'm my grandfather, she thought, the botanist.

As Deva returned back to life, she made a home of John's house. The bathroom was feminized with rows of unguents, sweet scents, and stashes of tampons. Fluffy towels were introduced. John had never thought to replace his old, harsh ones. The kitchen was stocked and equipped for a more varied menu. Flowers inside the house became commonplace, not just once in fifteen years. The washing machine experienced a busier and more vivid life with Deva's and Nadia's brighter clothes, not just John's browns and grays. Nadia's possessions, her games, her books, her gadgets, had an irrepressible vitality of their own, spreading everywhere, forever multiplying and rarely being limited. John stepped back and let all this happen. Against his rules, Sunny was quickly corrupted into sleeping on Nadia's bed, and soon he allowed the same corruption of his own. And, finally, John's early imaginings for retirement came true: farm animals. A few chickens, some geese, a donkey, two goats, all instruments of greater happiness. Through this time, Deva's sadness about Harry shaded from loss into gratitude.

John let Deva take over. He let relax the reins of control, his settled daily disciplines, and found he liked this better. He learned to watch and listen for the changing moods of the others, and their shifting needs. He knew what this was: the miracle of another chance. In his seventies, out of nowhere, he had been washed clean and given this, a family he could attend to with kindness, even if his present kindness would never quite erase the punch back then. Nor would Deva's and Nadia's full embrace of him ever quite remove the echo of Veronica's accu-sation. Not quite, but almost.

The past turned out to want nothing from them. Gwen did not contact John again, nor did he contact her. He no longer studied foreign affairs to hold himself in readiness for a call to action. Deva heard nothing from London, not from

Professor Grinnell with his unhealthy interest in her, nor from his unpleasant friends in secret places. The past appeared to be embarrassed, and to have turned its back.

In time, Deva made some new friends, the mothers of other children at Nadia's school. Life grew. Someone put her in contact with the university, and she was invited to visit a class on Brazil. When news of her singing and academic achievements spread, she was invited to teach her own course on Brazilian culture. There were a few other Brazilians around, who led her to other foreign friends, and she once again found herself sitting at the table of lively international women at Omar's Bookstore Café, an established local now. She was laughing again. Men lingered, and though they were just men, not Harry, they were not bad men, and seemed to Deva not entirely beyond future consideration.

Ignoring Sunny's reproachful sigh, John now pushed open the door to Omar's, his attention bending towards the table of women. He saw Deva surrounded by her friends, in her new life that included him. It was Saturday morning and Nadia was there too, the star. Someone at the table saw him, waved, and called out, "Hi, John." Then there was this simple thing, of walking up to the table of good-natured, good people, who looked up towards him and smiled in welcome. The faces changed from year to year, but he recognized most of them. He approached slowly, unwrapping layers of deep pleasure that the others could not imagine: the waving, the smiles, the repeating of his name, now Nadia and Deva turning towards him, now Nadia reaching for his hand to draw him in.

Nadia explained him to the newcomer next to her. "This is my grandad. My mom's dad."

"Your mom?"

"Oh, this is my mom." Nadia reached out her other hand to Deva.

"I'm Deva," said Deva, leaning forward into view.

"Diva, like opera?"

"No, with an *e*. Long story. Brazilian story."

"But she does sing," someone said. "Sometimes Deva sings right here. In the café."

"Like an angel," offered a woman from Nigeria. "You must hear her."

A chair was found for John, who was hesitating. "Sit," commanded Deva. "I'll go and order your coffee."

"But," he objected, "this is the women's table."

"And we are honored," said an Indian woman. "We will gossip about you later."

"He's really your father? He doesn't look so Brazilian," the newcomer asked Deva.

"But he really is my father," said Deva, laughing.

The woman looked from one to the other, and took in Nadia too. "Okay, I can see it," she said.

"I lost him for a long time," said Deva. "Now I keep him close."

"I remember you from years ago," the Indian woman said to John. "You sat alone. You didn't smile in those days. People thought you unfriendly. But I thought you were handsome. We made up bad stories about you."

"I didn't have these two to make me smile," he explained.

"Sunny too," said Nadia.

"Yes, Sunny too," he agreed, looking through the window to where Sunny was surrounded by a gaggle of school girls.

John accepted the pleasure of attention. Today, no one was imagining an unsavory past for him. No one today had yet thought to ask where Nadia's father was in all this, but when they did, Deva would reply that he had been a wonderful man who had sadly passed away, and would not be able to distinguish in her heart whether she spoke of Andy, or of Harry.